— A *Kit* MYSTERY —

DANGER
AT THE ZOO

by Kathleen Ernst

American Girl

Visit our Web site at **americangirl.com**

Printed in China.
05 06 07 08 09 10 LEO 12 11 10 9 8 7 6 5 4 3 2 1

PICTURE CREDITS
The following individuals and organizations have generously given
permission to reprint illustrations contained in "Looking Back":
pp. 174–175—tiger exhibit, courtesy of the Cincinnati
Zoo & Botanical Garden; zoo entrance, courtesy of Kathleen Ernst;
pp. 176–177—zoo entrance, courtesy of Kathleen Ernst; caged lions,
Library of Congress; monkey house, courtesy of the Cincinnati
Zoo & Botanical Garden; pp. 178–179—Susie the gorilla with trainer
and Sol Stephan with elephant, courtesy of the Cincinnati Zoo &
Botanical Garden; pp. 180–181—newspaper clipping, courtesy
of the Cincinnati Zoo & Botanical Garden; barless lion exhibit,
courtesy of Kathleen Ernst; modern zoo exhibit,
photo by Jamie Young.

Illustrations by Jean-Paul Tibbles

Cataloging-in-Publication Data
available from the Library of Congress.

For every girl
who dreams of
being a writer

TABLE OF CONTENTS

1
A DREAM COME TRUE

Kit Kittredge took a deep breath as she paused outside the big brick building that housed Cincinnati's newspaper office. *Maybe today my dream of becoming a reporter will begin to come true!* she thought. Squaring her shoulders, she opened the door and began climbing the stairs.

When Kit pushed open the door to the newspaper office, she felt right at home. *Click, clackety, click!* Half a dozen people sat at cluttered desks, pounding on typewriters. Others were talking on telephones, and somewhere another phone was ringing. Kit breathed in the energy, wanting nothing more than to be a part of it.

"Hello, Kit!" a young woman at the

closest desk said with a smile, although her fingers didn't stop dancing over the type-writer keys. "Dropping off another letter for the editor?"

"Not this time," Kit answered happily. "Today I have a *meeting* with the editor!"

She found Mr. Gibson, the editor, talking on the telephone, alternately tapping his pencil against his desktop and scribbling notes. Gibb, as the reporters called him, always seemed busy with about six things at once. As Kit waited a polite distance away, she imagined herself busy behind her own desk, a story half-written, the telephone ringing. "This is Kit Kittredge," she'd say, snatching the phone with one hand while jotting notes with the other. "I've got a five o'clock deadline. Let's get to work."

Then Gibb slammed the phone down and waved her into a chair in front of his desk. "Good morning, sir," she said as she sat down.

"What? Oh, yes. 'Morning." He shuffled through some papers on his desk, then found

2

what he was looking for. "I got your letter."

Kit tried not to squirm with excitement. A week earlier she'd sent a letter to Mr. Gibson. She had reminded him about the positive responses he'd had regarding several letters to the editor she'd written, and about an essay competition she'd won. "I just finished fifth grade," the letter had concluded. "I'm a hard worker, and I know I'll make a good reporter one day. If you assign me to work with one of your reporters this summer, I can run errands or take notes or anything else. I can help the newspaper and learn at the same time." She hadn't dared hope he'd actually respond. But here she was!

Gibb squinted at the letter. "None of my reporters has time to take you on as an assistant."

Kit's heart sank.

"But I do have another project in mind," he continued.

Kit sat up very straight. "Yes, sir?"

"As you know," Gibb said, "we have a ladies' page with recipes, fashion tips, and garden ideas. We can spare some room in the corner for a children's piece."

"A children's piece?" Kit asked.

Gibb drummed his fingers on his desk: *brmm.* "People will eat it up—a story for young people, by a girl their own age."

Kit could hardly believe her ears. "Do you mean . . . I'll get to *write* the piece? My own *column?* Oh, Mr. Gibson, thank you!"

He snorted. "We'll give it a try. That's all I can promise."

Kit's mind raced. "I've met some children at the soup kitchen. And others at the hobo camps out by Union Station. They have fascinating stories—"

"No, no, no." Gibb waved her ideas aside. "We have plenty of gloomy stories already! I want birthday parties." *Brmm.* "Pony rides at the Zoological Garden." *Brmm.* "The Girls' Hobby Fair. I want fun. I want wholesome. You get the idea." *Brmm.* "People will love it."

Kit nodded firmly. "Yes, sir. I understand."

"Now, let's see. Today is Thursday, June

4

twentieth . . ." He squinted at a calendar. "Get your first piece here on Monday, July first. That gives you about ten days. Don't go over two hundred and fifty words. If it works out, we'll try it weekly. I'll give you a dollar for every story we print."

A whole dollar? Kit wanted to jump out of her chair.

Gibb's mouth twitched in a brief smile. *"And* your own byline."

Kit pictured her first story, with "By Kit Kittredge" printed beneath it. At that, she *did* jump out of her chair. She didn't quite dare hug Gibb, but she held out her hand. When he took it, she gave his a hearty shake. "Yes, sir!"

Gibb gave her a piece of paper. "Here's a letter of introduction that proves you're working for me. And remember, I want tight, polished writing." Before Kit could answer, the phone on his desk rang, and he snatched the receiver. "Gibson here. What? I just sent a man down there—*what?* I already said no to that . . ."

Kit knew her meeting with the editor was

over. Slipping the letter into her pocket, she headed toward the door. Before leaving, she took a last glance at the bustling office. She savored the sound of typewriters, the hum of conversation, the faint smell of ink and coffee. *I'm on my way!* she thought. This children's assignment was just the first step. One day, she'd be working on real news stories.

The June afternoon was sticky-hot, but Kit almost skipped home. She had an assignment, and a byline! She would have done the work for free, but she'd be getting paid, too. Money was tight for her family, and she loved the idea of being able to help with bills.

Her head was already brimming with story ideas. When her friend Ruthie got back from vacation, Kit could interview her about traveling all the way to the Grand Canyon.

Another good friend, a boy named Stirling, boarded at Kit's house because his family had lost their home in the Depression. Stirling had a part-time job selling newspapers, and he'd recently joined a special Boy Scout troop called the Zoo Guides. Kit thought giving tours at Cincinnati's Zoological Garden sounded like great fun, but the guide positions were open only to boys. *Maybe I can't be one of the Zoo Guides,* she thought, *but I can write a newspaper story about them!* That was even better.

❧

Kit bounded up the back steps. She could hardly wait to tell Mother about Gibb's offer. She skidded to a stop on the porch to give her dog, Grace, a friendly greeting. A low rumble of voices drifted through the kitchen window. That was odd—the kitchen was Mother's place, and the boarders usually didn't gather there. "I'll see you later, Grace," Kit promised.

Inside, she found Mother and Stirling sitting at the kitchen table with a young man, not yet twenty. He wore patched, dusty clothes and held a tattered cap. "Hello, Kit," he said.

Kit's eyes went wide. "Will Shepherd! Is it really you?"

"It's me." He stood up, extended a hand, and gave her own a firm shake.

"It's so good to see you!" Kit stepped back and looked him up and down. "You look different. But the same, too."

He shrugged. "It's been almost two years since I passed through Cincinnati."

"I got the postcards you sent from California and Oklahoma! They're pinned up on my wall." Kit plopped down at the table and leaned forward on her elbows. "Tell me all about your adventures!"

Kit and her family had met Will two years earlier, in the summer of 1933, when he'd passed through Cincinnati looking for work. After his family's farm in Texas had failed, Will had left home and become a hobo, traveling in empty freight-train cars, always searching for his next job.

Will smiled. He looked older than Kit remembered. Tiny lines near his eyes told her he'd spent too many hours squinting into the sun. New shadows in those eyes said he'd seen

8

plenty of hard times along the way. But he didn't talk about those. Instead he spoke of friends he'd met while picking grapes and digging potatoes and harvesting apples.

"I'm going to try my luck in the southeast," Will finished. "Georgia, or maybe Florida."

Kit sighed. "So you're just passing through again?"

"I've got to find work," Will said simply. "But I couldn't pass through Cincinnati without visiting you folks."

Kit glanced at her mother. "We could use some help in the vegetable garden."

Mother smiled. "Yes, indeed. If you wouldn't mind helping out for a day or so, we'd enjoy your company. I can't pay you, but you'd get three square meals a day."

"It would be my pleasure," Will said. "I really need to find a paying job, though. I ran into a fellow from my part of Texas a few weeks ago and got word of my folks. They've moved in with my uncle's family. It must be a strain for everyone. And my mama's sick."

Will clamped his mouth shut, but Kit could imagine his worry. People without enough to eat had no money to spare for doctor visits.

"Hey," Stirling said, "there's a job open at the zoo! When I was there this afternoon for my Zoo Guide training, I heard that one of the workers who cleaned cages has moved away."

"Work at a zoo?" Will scratched his ear. "Well, that's a new one. I sure don't have any experience like that. Still . . . I did grow up on a farm. I've shoveled out plenty of stalls in my day." He nodded. "I'll head right over and apply for the job. If I can talk them into giving me a chance, I know I can prove myself."

"Good for you!" Kit said. She liked Will's determination.

"I can show you where to go," Stirling offered. "We should hurry, before anyone else hears about the job."

Will cleaned up on the back porch. Then Kit and Mother waved as Stirling and Will strode away. "I hope Will gets the job," Kit said.

"I hope so, too," Mother said. Then she

looked at Kit. "What happened at the newspaper office?"

Kit explained her assignment. "It's even better than I hoped! I'll get a byline—and get paid, too!"

"Oh, Kit!" Mother clasped her hands. "You've always dreamed of becoming a reporter, and now it's about to happen."

Mother's praise made Kit's cheeks grow warm. "Well, not really," Kit said. "A *real* reporter writes about important things. About what this Depression is doing to good people, or about how much some kindness can mean to someone who's down on his luck."

"Everyone has to start somewhere," Mother said gently. "Writing these children's stories will be good experience, don't you think?"

"Oh, yes!" Kit didn't want Mother to think she was ungrateful for the opportunity Gibb had given her. "And I'll earn a dollar for every story. I'll be able to help out with bills."

"That will be lovely," Mother said. "Although you're already an enormous help, you know.

Come back inside, and we'll start getting ready for dinner."

As she followed her mother, Kit's mind lingered on Mr. Gibson's offer. She'd write the children's stories, but why not do some serious reporting, too? She could even surprise Gibb by turning in two stories—the assigned children's piece *and* an exciting news feature! She smiled, imagining Gibb handing her *two* dollars. She could use the extra money she'd earn for something special, like helping people who'd lost their jobs in the Depression, or calling her brother Charlie in Montana, where he was working.

Kit smacked a fist against her palm. It was a great plan! She just needed to borrow Will's can-do attitude and prove to Gibb that she was capable of reporting *real* news.

❧

Will and Stirling burst into the kitchen just as Kit and Mother began arranging food on serving platters. Kit took one look at Will's face and grinned. "You got the job!" she guessed.

"I got the job." Will's eyes danced with satisfaction—and relief.

"Now you'll have a regular paycheck!" Kit cheered. "And you can stay with us!"

"Kit, that's up to Will," Mother said. "Although you are welcome here, Will."

"Charlie's still in Montana, so you can have his bed on the sleeping porch upstairs!" Kit told Will hopefully. Having Will around would help make up for Charlie being so far away.

"Or you can share my room!" Stirling offered. "My mother is away visiting her sister."

Will looked from one to the other. "Those are two mighty fine offers, but I'm none too comfortable sleeping under a roof anymore. I'd figured to stay out at the rail yard with some of my friends." He chewed his lower lip. "How 'bout I take meals here and sleep out on the back porch?"

"It's settled!" Kit announced happily. Grabbing Will's hand, she led him around the kitchen in a boisterous version of the Texas two-step. "See, Will? I remember the dance you taught us. And can you show me and Stirling more symbols from the hoboes' secret code? And maybe help me practice my baseball pitch sometimes? And—"

"Kit!" Mother protested. "Give Will a chance to settle in. And remember, his job comes first."

"I don't mind, ma'am. But there is one thing." Will rubbed his palms on his trousers. "I won't get paid for two weeks . . ."

"We can work something out," Mother said calmly. "Starting right now. Wash up for supper, Will, and then come meet our other boarders."

When everyone was gathered around the big dining-room table, Kit made the introductions. "You probably remember Mr. Peck."

"Of course!" Will smiled. "You play that big fiddle." Mr. Peck and his bass fiddle had boarded with the Kittredges ever since they'd opened their doors.

Kit paused by the chair of one of their newest boarders, a pencil-thin young woman with big dark eyes. "This is Miss Bravetti." Kit always rolled the name from her tongue with her best Italian accent—Br-r-ra-VET-ti— hoping it would coax a smile from the shy teacher. Kit thought anyone with such a dramatic name should be bold and fun-loving, but Miss Bravetti crept around the house as if she were afraid of her own shadow. "She's only been here a month," Kit told Will. "She teaches English at the high school."

Will nodded. "How do."

Miss Bravetti managed a quick smile in return.

"And this is Mrs. Dalrymple." Kit rolled the r's in this name too, just for fun.

"Ma'am," Will said. With his Texas accent, it sounded like "may-um."

"Mrs. Dalrymple moved in with us after her husband passed away," Kit added. "She makes beautiful quilts."

"Idle hands are the devil's workshop, I always say." Mrs. Dalrymple looked quite satisfied with herself. "That reminds me,

Mrs. Kittredge. The next time my quilting-circle friends come, we'll need to move some furniture out of the way so we can put up the quilting frame in the living room. Now, Will." She peered at him over round, black-rimmed glasses. "I imagine this job at the zoo will keep you out of trouble."

"Yes, ma'am," Will said politely. Standing safely behind Mrs. Dalrymple, Kit rolled her eyes at Stirling. The plump, no-nonsense widow took some getting used to.

"Please, everyone, don't let the food get cold," Mother said. "My husband is working late tonight." After losing his car dealership several years ago, Mr. Kittredge had finally found part-time employment at the airport. The work wasn't steady, but he was glad to have it.

While they ate, Will told them about his interview. "After talking to the head keeper, I had to meet Sol Stephan, the superintendent." He reached for a biscuit. "I'll start out working the late shift, from noon to nine."

Stirling beamed at Will. "We both have work to do at the zoo!"

"Why, so do I," Mr. Peck said. "The orchestra is accompanying the Zoo Opera every week, and we're planning a big concert for the Fourth of July. That's just two weeks from tonight!"

"I have a big announcement, too!" Kit exclaimed. She told the boarders about her newspaper assignment and smiled proudly as they congratulated her. "I thought I'd start by writing an article about Stirling and the Zoo Guides," she added.

Stirling almost choked on a bite of ham salad. "Does that have to be your *first* story? I'm still in training! I don't want a reporter along on my very first real tour of the monkey house next week!"

Kit laughed. She didn't feel like a real reporter yet, but she was pleased that her friend had given her that title. "I can hold off on that, I guess. I'll just have to find another story for my first article."

"I saw a poster downtown about a children's

pet show being held this weekend," Mr. Peck said. "That might make a good story."

"That's a great idea." Kit nodded. "I'll start with that." *And in the meantime,* she thought, *I'll start looking for my* real *news story.*

2
TROUBLE AT THE ZOO

After breakfast the next day, Will offered Kit a game of catch. Kit grabbed her mitt, tossed Will the ball, and raced to the backyard. "Go ahead—fire a good one," she called. She loved the sound of the baseball hitting her mitt, the smell of the leather, even the *smack* of a solid catch vibrating into her hand.

"Hey, good catch!" Will called. "Maybe you should be a sports reporter!"

"I'd rather cover the news." Kit sent Will her best fastball. Darn—it went wide. She *was* out of practice. Then Will wound up for another pitch, and she forgot all about reporting for a while.

"I've got to call it quits," Will said finally. "I told your mother I'd do some gardening this morning, and I sure don't want to be late for my first day on the job."

"Thanks for playing, Will," Kit said. Grace, dozing on the back porch, thumped her tail as they approached. "Even Grace is glad you're back." Will punched Kit playfully in the arm before going to see what Mother needed.

It's funny, Kit thought as she went inside, *how so many of the people who stay at our boarding house start feeling like family.* That thought gave her an idea, and she climbed the stairs to the second floor and knocked on one of the doors. It opened at once. "Oh, Kit!" Miss Bravetti said. She took a deep breath. "I was about to go out."

"I wanted to talk with you about something," Kit said. "But if it's a bad time, I can come back later."

"No, no, I was just going for a walk. That can wait. Please, come in." Miss Bravetti gestured Kit into the room.

To economize, Mrs. Dalrymple and Miss Bravetti had agreed to share a bedroom.

Photographs, a jewelry box, quilting patterns, and sewing supplies cluttered Mrs. Dalrymple's dresser and nightstand. In sharp contrast, Miss Bravetti's dresser top and nightstand were bare. The only keepsake Kit had ever seen was the heart-shaped pin Miss Bravetti always wore. Kit, who dusted the bedroom every Saturday, had always been grateful for that! But it seemed sad, too.

"What can I do for you, Kit?" Miss Bravetti's fingers plucked nervously at her skirt.

Kit perched on the bed. "Since you're an English teacher, I hoped you might give me some advice about my newspaper articles."

"Oh!" Miss Bravetti looked relieved. "I'd be happy to help you, Kit. I've never worked for a newspaper, but I do teach journalism to my senior students. Do you have an article you'd like me to read?"

"I haven't gotten that far," Kit confessed. "I'm going to write a story about that pet show. That's due a week from Monday. I also want to write a serious news story. The thing is . . ."

Kit idly tapped her heel against the bedpost. "I don't know where to find a real news story. I want to write about something that another reporter hasn't already covered."

Miss Bravetti nodded, looking thoughtful. "Perhaps you should begin by thinking about your goals for this serious news story. Do you want to share information about a problem, so your readers will get involved? Or perhaps help readers imagine something exciting by reading your story? If you know what you want to accomplish, it will be easier to know where to look."

"I hadn't thought about anything like that," Kit admitted. "Do all reporters think so much before they start writing?"

Miss Bravetti smiled. "I don't know, but I suspect the good ones do. Writing a great story is the last step in a long process."

"Really?" Kit loved to pound away at her old typewriter or scribble stories in notebooks. But those stories were mostly about friends or family and were easy to write.

"Before you can write a good news story, you need to gather facts," Miss Bravetti said. "Reporters often interview people, or go to the library to look up information." Her eyes sparkled. "I imagine it must feel a bit like detective work. That's what good journalism is all about."

Detective work. Journalism. Kit loved the sound of those words. "Do you think reporters can tell right away when they've found a great story?" she asked. A great story—that's what she needed to impress Gibb!

"At first, they may not have more than a hunch. Sometimes writers have to trust their instincts."

"I'll think about that," Kit said. "Thanks, Miss Bravetti! I'll come back for more advice once I get started."

The sparkle disappeared from Miss Bravetti's eyes. "I . . . I might be out quite a bit," she said. "I'm hoping to find a summer job, you see, and I'm tutoring—"

"That's okay," Kit interrupted. She felt a bit

embarrassed—here she was asking for Miss Bravetti's time when other students were paying for it!

Miss Bravetti put a hand on Kit's arm. "But anytime I'm home, I'd be happy to talk with you. You can always ask me for help. All right?"

"All right," Kit said, partly in agreement and partly to quiet the worry that had once again puckered Miss Bravetti's forehead. "I will."

❧

"Hey, Kit," Stirling called on Sunday evening, poking his head through the doorway of her attic bedroom. "How was the pet show? Are you writing about it?"

Kit pounded out one more word on her black typewriter. "It was fun, and I took lots of good notes. Two boys even had baby alligators on display!"

Stirling leaned over her shoulder. "*Perilous,*"

he read. *"Fraught with danger.* Gee, Kit, I don't know. That sounds too dramatic for a pet show, even one with baby alligators!"

"This isn't about the pet show." Kit told Stirling about her plan to submit two articles to Gibb. "I sat down to work on the pet show story, but my mind keeps jumping to the *real* news story I want to write. Miss Bravetti said I should set goals for my news article, and right now I'm making a list of words and phrases I want to use. I want to investigate something that requires some real detective work, so I can write an *exciting* story."

Stirling cocked his head. "Where are you going to find a big story like that?"

"I haven't figured that out yet," Kit admitted.

"Why don't you come to the zoo tomorrow afternoon?" Stirling suggested. "It's an exciting place."

Kit loved the Zoological Garden as much as anyone in Cincinnati. But was the zoo a perilous place, fraught with danger? Hardly!

Still, she didn't want to disappoint her friend, and she could start researching her story about the Zoo Guides. "Sounds great," she said. "I'll be there."

❧

As Kit approached the zoo entrance at the corner of Vine Street and Erkenbrecher Avenue on Monday afternoon, she saw a handful of men walking back and forth in front of the ticket gate. They held picket signs proclaiming "Zoo Management Unfair!" and "Fair Work Deserves Fair Pay!"

Stirling, waiting patiently on the curb, waved when he saw her. "Hey, Kit! You're right on time."

"What's all that about?" Kit asked, nodding toward the men with signs.

"They're on strike," Stirling said in a low voice. "Those men don't think the zoo managers are treating them fairly, so they stopped working."

Kit watched the strikers for a moment. "Do you think they're right?" she asked.

"It's just a few of the workers," Stirling told her. "Most of the workers I've talked to are happy with their jobs."

The zoo visitors passing through the entrance gate shot the men uneasy glances and kept their distance. *People have too many troubles of their own to get involved in new ones,* Kit thought.

"Come on." Stirling headed toward the gate. "I told Will we'd meet him on his break."

"Great!" Kit shrugged out of the book bag she used to carry her notebook and pencil and swung it by the straps. "You gave your first tour today, right? How did it go?"

"Pretty well! The keepers gave us lots of information last week, and practicing our talks on other guides helps a lot." Stirling waved at a man by the gate who wore a brown uniform with a shoulder patch that identified him as Zoo Police. "Hello, Officer Culpepper!" he called.

Officer Culpepper was a big man with hair that reminded Kit of spilled salt and pepper. His feet were planted like oak trees; his arms were folded across his chest as if he dared anyone to cause trouble. "I thought you were headed home, lad. Did you forget about a tour?"

Stirling smoothed the crisply ironed shirt of his Zoo Guides uniform. "I came out to meet my friend. This is Kit. She's a newspaper reporter."

Kit held out Gibb's letter of introduction with a flush of pride. "It's good to meet you, sir. I'm researching an article I'm going to write about the Zoo Guides."

"Well, now, lookee here." A smile briefly softened the officer's face as he scanned the letter. "Doesn't that just beat the band!"

"Officer Culpepper is the head of the Zoo Police," Stirling explained.

"I didn't know the zoo needed its own policemen," Kit said, glancing over her shoulder. "Is it because of the strike?"

"That's mostly been peaceable," Officer

28

Culpepper said, although Kit noticed his gaze shifting constantly over the men with picket signs. "I hear the strikers are about to reach an agreement with the zoo managers. Still, there will probably be one or two grumblers unhappy with the settlement."

"I suppose so." Kit didn't know what to make of the strike. She certainly believed that all workers deserved fair wages. She also knew that ever since the Depression started, the zoo had been so desperate for funds that many people in Cincinnati had feared the zoo would close and the animals would be sold.

"And with all the concerts and special activities held in the evenings, we get our share of troublemakers," Officer Culpepper added. "Pickpockets. Boys making mischief. Not to mention your everyday bum." His steel gaze suddenly fixed on a small, shabby man slowly approaching the gate. The man's black hair touched his collar, and his jacket—a startling cherry red—badly needed mending. The policeman strode toward the smaller man and waved an imposing hand. "Away with you!"

A torrent of words exploded from the man's mouth. "What language is that?" Kit whispered to Stirling.

"Beats me," Stirling said. "But I'm pretty sure it's not German or Italian."

Kit listened hard. She thought she heard a few heavily accented English words jumbled into the man's protests, but she couldn't make out what he was saying.

Officer Culpepper grabbed the man's arm and turned him away. "I've told you before, it costs a quarter to get in. No quarter, no ticket. Now, don't hang around here bothering good folks. Go find a soup kitchen." The officer waited until the man had shuffled away before turning back to Stirling and Kit. "You kids go on in." He waved them through the gate.

"I feel guilty coming in for free when that poor man got turned away," Kit murmured to Stirling. "It looked like he's out of work. He probably just wanted to see the animals and forget his troubles for a while."

"Maybe." Stirling looked at the ground, and Kit wondered if he was thinking of his father, who had disappeared after losing his own job.

"Well, I'm going to think about that," Kit said briskly. "Maybe the zoo can let poor people in for free one day a month."

"That's a good idea." Stirling smiled. "Come this way. We're going to meet Will by the monkey house."

Trees and elaborate flower gardens dotted the zoo's sprawling acres. Most of the animals could be seen from a main trail that circled the grounds. Smaller trails crisscrossing the center of the park led to more animal exhibits, the concert pavilion, and the restaurant.

Stirling and Kit turned left and wandered along the west side of the zoo. "This is the shortest route to the monkey house," Stirling said. "Hey, there's Bob—he's giving tours by the new lion and tiger grottoes this summer. Hi, Bob!" Stirling waved but didn't stop talking. "You should really take the time to

31

see the new grottoes. They're barless exhibits where animals live in natural areas instead of cages. The lions and tigers are over that way." He gestured.

Kit didn't remind him that she knew the zoo grounds almost as well as he did. Before the Depression, her family had come here often. She smiled, remembering elephant rides with Charlie, and cold lemonade and concerts. Her sadness slipped away. The sunshine draped her shoulders like a soft sweater. Distant carousel music mingled with children's squeals and the piercing cry of a peacock nearby. The air smelled of roasted peanuts and dirty straw. Two boys jostled her as they pounded down the path toward the bison pen. Kit remembered racing her brother down this same path.

"And here's my area!" Stirling announced proudly, turning right. Kit recognized the monkey house ahead. The elegant gray building, crowned with a red dome, stood on a slope inside the main loop trail.

"Some of the smaller monkeys have access to

both inside and outside cages in the summer."
Stirling nodded toward a tall outdoor cage
attached to one side of the building. Visitors
leaned over the safety fence, tossing peanuts
through the bars at the animals romping inside.
"Those little ones with white faces are squirrel
monkeys," he added. "There's an outdoor
spider monkey cage on the other side of the
building. And the keepers moved a group of
rhesus monkeys to monkey island last week."
He pointed to a path that led to the edge of a
small pond with an island in the middle. Kit
saw nimble monkeys scampering playfully
on the island. "They'll live on the island all
summer. They're very lively, so they're real
favorites with the visitors."

Kit grinned. "You got assigned to a great
area."

"I know!"

They sat on a shaded bench near the outdoor
squirrel monkey cage to wait for Will. A few
minutes later he appeared on the path leading
from the nearby aviaries, which housed the

zoo's famous collection of wild birds. "Hey, you two!" he called. After sitting on the ground beside them, he pulled a handkerchief from his pocket and mopped his forehead. "Whew! It's a hot one today."

Kit could tell from the sweat and dirt staining Will's shirt that he'd been working hard. "How do you like your new job, Will?"

"Just fine." Will pushed his cap back on his head. "It's a lot more interesting than picking peas all day. I like being around the animals."

"Is it scary?" Kit asked eagerly, imagining Will tiptoeing around lions and elephants. "Do you get to handle some of the animals?"

He smiled. "I don't do much but clean cages."

"Soon there won't even be so many cages," Stirling added. "As they build more barless exhibits . . ." His voice trailed away as wooden tires crunched on the path, and a small pony cart emerged from the trees. "It's the superintendent!" he breathed.

Kit couldn't help staring at the white-haired man driving the cart. In spite of the sticky heat, he wore a black suit coat, vest, and tie over a starched white shirt. A formal black derby sat squarely on his head. His back was straight and his white mustache bristled. As the pony clip-clopped nearer, the man looked sharply at Kit, Stirling, and Will. He clucked to the pony and stopped the cart in front of their bench. "Mr. Shepherd!" he exclaimed.

Will scrambled to his feet, snatching his cap from his head. "Yes, sir!"

"I understand you had late duty in this area last night. Is that true?"

"Yes, sir," Will said again. "I left a little after nine o'clock."

Kit and Stirling exchanged puzzled glances. Something in Mr. Stephan's tone made Kit uneasy.

"I checked the monkey house doors last night at twenty past nine," the superintendent said. "The main door was unlocked."

Will frowned and rubbed his forehead with

his fingertips. "But . . . but I locked it before I left! I'm sure I did—"

"Locks don't open themselves," the superintendent said crisply. "And I don't tolerate carelessness. Is that understood?"

A curious squirrel monkey leapt to the closest bars of the outdoor cage, making small chittering sounds. Kit held her breath. "Yes, sir," Will said finally.

Superintendent Stephan nodded, and his voice warmed a few degrees. "That's good, son. Just be more careful next time." He slapped the lines lightly against the pony's back, and the cart lurched forward.

The pony cart rattled around a bend and out of sight. Stirling finally broke the awkward silence. "Don't mind, Will," he said. "Everybody makes mistakes—"

Will shook his head. "I locked that door. I'm sure I did."

"Maybe you thought you did, but the latch didn't quite catch," Stirling offered.

Will didn't answer. His tired smile was gone.

Kit saw the tight set to his jaw and the shadows back in his eyes.

Finally Will shoved his cap back on his head. "I've got to get back to work," he said, and strode away.

3
INSTINCTS

Stirling shook his head. "Anyone could make a mistake like that. I'm sure it will soon be forgotten."

Kit hoped so. From the look in Will's eyes, however, she suspected that he wouldn't forget his scolding any time soon.

Kit and Stirling sat for a few moments longer as the last weary visitors wandered past. Kit knew that the zoo's fancy restaurant was still open, and no doubt an opera performance or band concert or puppet show was scheduled for the evening, but the animal exhibits closed at five o'clock. Soon the paths became quiet. A worker trundled a wheelbarrow of dirty straw from the monkey house. Two more workers passed, hauling buckets of water.

"Come on," Stirling said finally. "Let's go inside, and I'll show you around."

"You're sure we're allowed?" Kit asked.

Stirling nodded. "I'm sure. The Zoo Guides are allowed to stay after hours. Learning how the keepers do their work is part of our training. And you're here on newspaper business."

They climbed stone steps to the monkey house's main door. Kit looked down the familiar hallway to the center of the building, where a circular open space surrounded by marble columns soared up to the two-storied dome. Huge cages lined the hallways that led out from the rotunda, but safety railings kept visitors from getting too close to the animals.

Kit was used to hearing happy shrieks and laughter bounce off the high ceiling, but now the building seemed strangely still. She dug her notebook and pencil out of her book bag and made a few notes before asking, "Can we visit Susie?"

Stirling grinned. "Sure! She's our most famous resident." He led Kit to a large cage near the building's side door. A huge gorilla squatted on the cement floor, poking her long fingers through some straw.

"She's glaring at us," Kit breathed, glad Susie was behind bars. A fascinated shiver ran down Kit's spine.

"Actually, most of the time she's quite friendly," said a voice near them. Kit whirled and saw a tall boy wearing a zookeeper's uniform. He stood in the barred passageway that separated Susie's cage from the chimpanzees' cage next to it. He held a bucket brimming with bananas, lettuce, and crusts of bread. A sprinkling of ginger-colored freckles over his nose and a gap between his two front teeth gave him a boyish look. Kit noticed the muscles in his arms and shoulders, though, and guessed he was a few years older than she was.

"Hi, Rudy!" Stirling said. "Meet my friend Kit. She's researching a newspaper article about the Zoo Guides program."

Rudy surveyed her with a friendly grin. "Hello, Kit!"

"Rudy works here." Stirling's voice held a hint of awe. "He's already an assistant keeper."

"Wow!" Kit made a note on her pad.

Rudy's shrug didn't quite hide his pride. "My dad was a keeper here until he died last year. I helped him from the time I could walk."

"Here in the monkey house?"

"I've worked all over the zoo, but the monkey house is my favorite," Rudy said. "The monkeys all have real personalities." He nodded toward the gorilla. "Susie and her trainer have dinner together every afternoon. The trainer sets a table with plates, cups, and spoons, and she sits down and eats polite as you please."

"Come back someday at four-thirty and see for yourself," Stirling added. "Everyone loves it."

Rudy nodded. "Susie's trainer has been with her since she was a baby. Susie thinks of him as a parent. No one else takes care of her. I can't imagine what she'd do without him."

"That's amazing!" Kit stared at the gorilla, impressed.

"I was just about to feed the chimpanzees,"

Rudy said. Using a key that hung from a ring on his belt, he unlocked a door to the chimps' cage.

Stirling pointed to the passageway between the cages. "Those passageways keep the animals separated from their neighbors," he explained. "And they would keep an animal contained if it managed to get out when the keeper opened the door."

Rudy slipped inside the chimpanzees' cage and latched the door firmly behind him. Half a dozen chimps scampered toward him, running on the soles of their feet and the knuckles of their hands. "I'm running a little late today, but Superintendent Stephan likes the keepers to tend the animals during public viewing hours whenever possible," he said. "He wants to educate visitors, not just entertain them." As Rudy scattered food across the floor, most of the chimpanzees snatched some dinner. "Hey, wait your turn," he called to a greedy chimp.

Kit watched with delight as the chimpanzees deftly peeled their bananas with long fingers. "They look like little people!"

One of them climbed nimbly into Rudy's arms. "I used to help my dad train chimps," he said affectionately. "This little fellow can roller-skate and ride a tricycle."

Kit pointed to a chimp squatting alone in one corner of the cage. "Is that one sick?"

Rudy sighed, put his chimpanzee friend down, and took a banana to the loner. "This is Buddy Boy. He's our newest chimp, and he hasn't settled in yet." Rudy held the banana out to him. "Come on, Buddy. Have some supper." The chimp grinned at Rudy, but he didn't take the banana. Rudy finally left it on the floor nearby.

"He can't be too unhappy," Kit observed. "He's smiling."

Rudy shook his head. "My dad always said that when chimpanzees grin like that, it really means they're anxious or afraid."

At least you have a home, Buddy Boy! Kit thought as Rudy let himself out of the chimps' cage. She remembered the crimson-jacketed man Officer Culpepper had turned away at the gate, and she wondered if he'd found his way to a soup kitchen.

A few moments later, Rudy joined Kit and Stirling in the public area. "I just need to update the chalkboard," he said. He ducked under the safety railing and jotted some notes about the afternoon feeding on a chalkboard attached to the front of the chimpanzees' cage. "These chalkboards give us another way to educate visitors," he explained. "Hey, want to see something pretty special? Come on."

Kit and Stirling followed the young assistant keeper to the back of the monkey house, directly across the rotunda from the main entrance. Rudy paused at a door marked *Workers Only!* and reached again for his big key ring. Kit exchanged a delighted look with Stirling. How exciting to get a glimpse behind the scenes!

They followed Rudy through the *Workers Only!* door and down a short hallway. Rudy opened a door on the left. "Come on into our veterinary room."

At first Kit noticed only the shiny examining

44

table, which almost filled the narrow room, and the crowded shelves that lined the walls, filled with bottles, instruments, bandages, and other supplies. Then she spotted a cage against the far wall. Inside crouched a small, red-faced, brown-furred monkey.

"Meet our smallest resident." Rudy knelt beside the cage. "See our baby rhesus monkey? This little guy is just three days old."

Kit gasped when she saw that the monkey she'd first noticed was cradling a tiny infant. Nestled in his mother's arms, the baby looked up at Kit with huge dark eyes, his expression almost human. After a moment he sighed and cuddled more closely against his mother. Kit's heart melted. "Ooh!" she whispered, crouching by the cage for a better look. "He could fit on the palm of my hand!"

"Superintendent Stephan wants to put him in a special exhibit as soon as we can," Rudy said. "Everyone loves the babies."

"Thank you, Rudy. What a treat!" Kit stood reluctantly.

Rudy wiped his hands on his trousers, then stuck his right hand out toward Kit. "It was good to meet you, Kit. I've gotta finish feeding the animals." He ushered her and Stirling back to the public hall.

"He seems nice," Kit said as Rudy walked away, whistling off-key.

Stirling nodded. "He is. He doesn't have any family, but the superintendent kept Rudy on after his father died."

"Superintendent Stephan is an interesting man," Kit mused. She'd glimpsed a strict supervisor disciplining Will, but Stirling spoke of a kindly man who kept an orphaned boy on his payroll.

Stirling headed toward the building's side entrance. "I think he knows that Rudy really loves the animals." Stirling pushed open the door. "That's what matters most—"

"Hey, watch it!" A young, sandy-haired man almost collided with them. Water from the large bucket he carried sloshed over the side and spattered his worn work boots.

"I'm sorry, Otis," Stirling said politely. "I didn't see you."

Otis's scowl reminded Kit of Susie the gorilla. "What are you kids doing here anyway?" Otis asked. "It's after hours. Get outta here."

Kit stepped back, surprised by the menace in his voice. He was short, but broad-shouldered and muscular.

Stirling sucked in a deep breath, then lifted his chin. "I'm sorry we bumped into you. But Zoo Guides are allowed to stay after the buildings close."

"I said, get *out* of here," Otis growled. "Or else." Then he stomped into the monkey house, slamming the door behind him.

"Phe-ew!" Kit exclaimed. "Who was that?"

Stirling looked disgusted. "Otis. He's an assistant keeper. They keep him on late shift because he's not good at answering visitors' questions."

"Is he always so cranky?" Kit asked, as they wandered on through the grounds.

"Who knows?" Stirling shrugged. "Rudy

told me Otis hasn't worked here very long."

They paused at the edge of the moat around monkey island. Kit watched as dozens of rhesus monkeys romped over the artificial rocks and scampered up and down two dead trees that had been secured on the island.

Kit smiled at their games, but her thoughts were tumbling. *I guess I expected visiting the zoo to feel just like it did when I was little,* she thought. Now her magical memories of the zoo were sharpened by images of striking workers and a penniless man outside the gate, and by scoldings and threats inside.

Had Stirling been right? Could it be that the big news story she'd been searching for was right here at the zoo? Kit decided she'd better keep her eyes and ears open. Maybe do a little detective work. *Trust your instincts,* Miss Bravetti had told her. Kit's instincts told her that something wasn't quite right at the zoo.

4
TROUBLE AT HOME

After lunch the next day, Mother asked Kit to run to the grocery store for some canned fish. When Kit got back, she found Mother sitting on the porch. The sound of women's voices came faintly through an open window. Kit didn't like the expression on Mother's face. "Is everything all right?"

Mother tipped her head toward the window. "Mrs. Dalrymple's quilting friends are in the living room." A burst of laughter from the quilters echoed from inside. "It's such an . . . *energetic* group."

Mother had once been an active member of a garden club. She'd spent her days tending phlox and roses and pansies in beds that flowed around the house, and she had often had her friends over for lovely luncheons. But she hadn't hosted the garden club in a very long time. Now much of the backyard had been converted to a vegetable garden, and her home was filled with boarders.

"That's not the only thing troubling me." Mother rubbed her forehead. "I put six loaves of bread out on the porch to cool this morning. When I came out to fetch them just now, there were only five."

"What?" Kit blinked, looking around. "Who would take a loaf of bread?"

"Some poor hungry soul, I suppose. Probably a hobo passing by." Mother sighed. "Your father left some snap peas in a basket on the back step, and about half of them are gone, too."

"Did you see anyone?" Kit asked.

"The kitchen felt like a train station for a while, with people coming and going. Miss Bravetti wanted a glass of water before she went out. Mr. Peck stopped to remind me that he has an early rehearsal tonight, and Mrs. Dalrymple came in to remind me that her quilting friends were coming over. A family of bears could have marched through the backyard without me noticing."

I wish I'd been here, Kit thought. *I'd have noticed!*

Mother stood. "Well, we won't starve for want of a loaf of bread and some peas. We'll make do with one loaf for dinner this evening, and then we'll be back on track. I just wish that whoever it was had knocked on the door and asked for food. We can always spare something."

Kit chewed her lip. "Did Grace bark?" she asked.

"Not so much as a friendly yip. She's really rather useless as a watchdog, I'm afraid." Mother put a hand on Kit's shoulder. "Come inside. We'll fix some tea for Mrs. Dalrymple's friends before she comes looking for it herself."

"I'll be right along," Kit said. She'd been thinking about Mother's comment: *I just wish they'd knocked on the door and asked for food.* It had reminded her of something.

Kit hurried to the back corner of the yard, where the fence met the street. And there it was—the figure of a cat, sketched in pencil on the fencepost. Will had shown it to her the first time he stopped at the Kittredges'. It was part of the hoboes' secret code and meant that a kind-hearted woman lived at that house. Someone had recently marked over it again. The lines were dark and clear. *Any hobo who saw that sign wouldn't be afraid to ask Mother for food,* she thought. So it seemed unlikely that the thief was a hobo.

But if a hobo hadn't stolen the food . . . who had?

❧

Later that afternoon, while Kit washed fresh baby carrots, Mother made codfish cakes from a recipe she'd found in the newspaper. "This 'Economical Dinner' menu feature is so helpful," she murmured, mixing leftover mashed potatoes with the canned fish. "I can count on these recipes to pinch pennies as hard as I do."

When I start earning money for my newspaper stories, maybe Mother won't have to pinch pennies quite so hard, Kit thought. *Or worry about one missing loaf of bread.* She could hardly wait to hand Mother her first dollar!

When everyone had settled at the dinner table, Kit circled the room slowly, carrying a tray that held individual plates of salad. Mother had sliced canned pears into strips and criss-crossed them over tiny leaves of fresh lettuce, with grape halves balanced on top. The effect was so pretty that Kit was sure no one would mind making do with single slices of bread.

They hadn't counted on Stirling, who slid into his chair just as the clock chimed six, still wearing his Zoo Guides uniform. "This bread is wonderful!" he raved. He popped the last bite into his mouth. "Is there more in the kitchen?"

Mother gave him a calm smile. "I'm afraid not."

Mrs. Dalrymple frowned. "Mrs. Kittredge! I love to bake, and I do miss having my own oven. Tomorrow, I'll help you in the kitchen."

Mother blinked. "Why, I . . . that is . . . that's really not necessary."

"Nonsense." Mrs. Dalrymple scooped a second codfish cake onto her plate. "I'm glad to do it. No need to thank me."

Mother looked as if she might be silently counting to ten. "Mrs. Dalrymple," she said after an awkward pause, "I appreciate your kind offer, but I really must keep track of supplies in the kitchen—"

"Of course, of course." Mrs. Dalrymple cut Mother off with a wave of her hand. "I'll furnish my own ingredients. And Angela can help me." She nodded toward Miss Bravetti.

Kit saw Mother glance helplessly at Dad, who gave a tiny, sympathetic hitch of his shoulders. Mother wasn't nearly as formal with the boarders as she used to be. Mrs. Dalrymple hadn't lived with the Kittredges very long, however, and no one was quite comfortable with her yet. *First Mrs. Dalrymple took over the living room,* Kit thought, *and now she wants to take over the kitchen, too.*

After dinner, Kit and Stirling cleared the table and did the dishes. Mrs. Dalrymple brought her sewing basket to the dining room. She pulled out squares pieced from colorful bits of fabric and started arranging them on the table. Kit had just begun to put plates back into the cupboard in the dining room when she heard footsteps clicking in the hall.

Mrs. Dalrymple craned her neck. "Is that you, Angela?" she called. "I would appreciate your help laying out these quilt blocks."

Miss Bravetti poked her head into the room. She was dressed to go out and held a perky straw hat in her hands. "I—I'm very sorry, Mrs. Dalrymple, but I have a teachers' meeting tonight."

"Hmph." Mrs. Dalrymple smoothed a piece of yellow fabric that had dared to wrinkle. "School is out, for heaven's sake! You could be spending your evening hours doing something more productive."

For a moment Kit thought Miss Bravetti was going to cry. "I—I'm sorry you don't think I'm being productive," she quavered. "But the other ladies expect me. This is just the women teachers, you see." She settled the hat on her head.

"Why just the women teachers?" Kit asked.

"Because we have unique problems!" Miss Bravetti burst out. "The school board came very close to firing all of the married women teachers last year because some people said it wasn't fair to pay wages to women who have husbands. And now the male teachers are fighting to be paid higher wages than we are!" Her voice was rising. "I'm a good teacher, and I'm struggling to make ends meet, too! I deserve my paycheck!" With that, she scurried from the room.

"Gosh!" Kit said. "I didn't mean to upset her! I was just curious."

"You asked a reasonable question," said Mrs. Dalrymple. "I gather that Angela comes from a strict home. I don't think her parents ever wanted her opinion, much less asked for it. It took great courage for her to move out on her own, which is why I've taken her under my wing."

Well . . . out on her own in a house full of people! Kit thought. She wondered if Mrs. Dalrymple's wing was sometimes a bit heavy for the teacher's thin shoulders.

Mrs. Dalrymple squinted at her rows of fabric squares and rearranged two of them. "*You* could help me with this, young lady."

"I was hoping to start working on my pet show story tonight," Kit said quickly. It was true—every time she planned to start writing it, she got distracted by something else.

"That's a beautiful pattern, ma'am," Stirling said as he put a cup away. "Does it have a name?"

"Dresden Plate." Mrs. Dalrymple adjusted a square, looking satisfied.

"The quilt will look lovely on your bed," Kit said, and she meant it. She didn't have the patience to cut scraps of fabric into tinier scraps, then sew them back together, but she admired the final effect.

Mrs. Dalrymple snorted. "It's not for me! This one's going to the soup kitchen. Poor people need pretty quilts more than I do— Oh, heavens, the stitches in this block are too long. If I've told the ladies once, I've told them a hundred times: nothing less than ten stitches to the inch."

As Mrs. Dalrymple started ripping out the seams, Kit caught Stirling's eye and jerked her head toward the stairs. Once they were safe in her attic bedroom, Kit plopped on her bed. "Phew! A narrow escape. Mrs. Dalrymple wears me out."

"Me, too."

Kit shook her head. "I shouldn't get too annoyed with her, though. Imagine putting all that work into a quilt, then giving it away to someone in need! That's a wonderful thing

to do. But listen—something happened today."
She told Stirling about the missing food.

Stirling shrugged. "As your mother said,
it was probably just a hungry hobo."

"So why didn't he just ask for food? The
'kind-hearted woman' sign is still on the
fence. And why didn't Grace bark? She's not
the fiercest watchdog in the world, but she
usually does bark a bit if a stranger comes
into the yard."

Stirling frowned. "But if a stranger didn't
. . ." His words trailed away, and he stared at
Kit. She could tell they were both thinking the
same thing.

If not a stranger, then . . . who?

5
DETECTIVE WORK

Kit walked to the zoo after lunch on Thursday. She hoped Stirling might let her come on one of his tours. Besides, she still had a hunch that her big news story might be found at the zoo, and she wanted to spend more time there.

As she headed down the main path, she saw Stirling and several other boys in Zoo Guides uniforms leaning on the fence by the zebra pen. Stirling waved and came to greet her. "Hey, Kit! I didn't know you were coming today."

"I thought I'd take more notes for my article," she told him. *Two* articles, if she was lucky!

Stirling took a deep breath. "You can come on one of my tours, if you want."

"Great. I will!" She nudged him with her

elbow. "I'll ask all kinds of strange questions."

"You'd better not! I've got exactly one week to get ready for the Fourth of July. Everyone says we'll have *huge* crowds that day. It's the biggest celebration of the summer." Stirling checked his watch. "Listen, I'm on a break. Rudy told me I could help him prepare the monkeys' afternoon meals. Want to come?"

Kit grinned. "Let's go!"

Inside the monkey house, they met Rudy by the *Workers Only!* door. He led them to a room across from the veterinary area. Apples, oranges, grapes, peanuts, celery, and yams were heaped on a long table in the center of the narrow room. Shelves around the walls held buckets, scoops, and cartons of cereal and bread. The room smelled of musty potatoes and rotting bananas.

"Wow!" Kit stared at the food. "It must be expensive to feed zoo animals. No wonder there was so much talk about closing the zoo when the Depression started."

Rudy put a bunch of grapes on a scale. "Every animal in the monkey house has a specific diet." He gestured toward a battered tin bowl holding two eggs and a pear. "That's for Buddy Boy, that new chimp. We're still trying to figure out what he likes."

"Do you know where Otis is?" Stirling asked. "I bet he'd holler if he found us in here."

Rudy's smile faded. "I don't care if Otis hollers. But there is something I should tell you."

"What?" Unease rippled over Kit's skin.

"Last night Officer Culpepper found the monkey house unlocked again."

Kit felt a sinking sensation in her stomach. "Was Will . . ."

Rudy nodded. "Will was the last one out." He scooped the grapes from the scale and dropped them into a bucket. "I'm sorry. I know he's your friend."

"Did he get fired?" Stirling asked anxiously.

"Not yet. But he got one mean talking-to when he came in at noon. Stirling, can you hand me some apples? I need six."

Will didn't do it! Kit thought, remembering the look in his eyes when Superintendent

DETECTIVE WORK

Stephan had scolded him on Monday.

"I want to talk to Will," she said as Stirling fetched the apples. "Do you know where he is?"

Rudy glanced at a clock on the wall. "I think he's cleaning cages at the aviaries. He'll probably take his supper break at five o'clock."

"Why don't you meet me again at four o'clock?" Stirling suggested to Kit. "You can come on my last tour, and then we can find Will when he goes on break. Do you mind hanging around for a couple of hours?"

"Not a bit!" Kit assured him. *I can put the time to good use*, she thought. Something strange was going on at the monkey house. It was time to do some investigating!

They left Rudy to his duties. After Stirling went to meet his next tour group, Kit stood for a moment in the monkey house's central rotunda. *Why*, she wondered, *would someone leave a door to this building open?* She was determined to figure out the puzzle.

The monkey house teemed with visitors.

Children darted from cage to cage. Stirling led his group inside and stopped at the orangutan cage. A little girl spilled her bag of peanuts and began to wail. Kit narrowed her eyes, trying to ignore the crowds and noise. She wanted to see the building as a troublemaker might.

Both the front door and the side door stood open on this hot afternoon, but she knew they'd be locked when the last worker left for the evening. She took a few moments to peer in every direction, searching for anything that seemed out of place or suspicious. No luck.

In the northeast corner of the building, by the baboons' cage, a narrow hallway led to one of the few areas not visible from the rotunda. Maybe that hidden corner held a clue! Trying hard to look casual, Kit wandered down the narrow hall. It led only to a door to the outside cage where the spider monkeys enjoyed the summer weather. Kit glanced over her shoulder before trying the door. It was securely locked.

A similar hallway in the southwest corner

led to the squirrel monkeys' outdoor cage.
Kit tried that door, too, with the same results.
"Well, that's good, I guess," Kit muttered.
A boy wearing horn-rimmed glasses gave her
a curious look. Kit decided she'd done all the
investigating inside that she could do without
attracting unwanted attention.

So what had she learned? *Not much,* Kit
thought as she headed out into the dazzling
sunshine. She hadn't seen anything suspicious
or noticed any other problems with security.
She had a clear picture of the layout of the
monkey house, but she still didn't know why
someone was unlocking a door at night.

That just means I need to do more investigating!
she thought. She was a reporter. It was her job
to sniff out trouble. She decided to look around
the zoo beyond the monkey house. She wasn't
sure what she was looking for, but she figured
she'd know it when she saw it!

Kit walked briskly down the slope toward the
main path that looped through the zoo grounds.
On the other side of that path, bordering the

outer edge of the zoo, were open pens for deer, elk, llamas, and camels. She stopped by a Zoo Guide who was just beginning a tour near the camel pen.

"Camels are sometimes called 'ships of the desert,'" he said earnestly. "They can carry as much as one thousand pounds . . ."

Kit stared across the camel pen, thinking more about Will's problems than about camels. The trouble just didn't make sense! Kit knew that the zoo's main entrance gate was locked securely at night by Officer Culpepper or one of the other zoo policemen. So, what was someone trying to accomplish by unlocking one of the monkey house doors at night? The only people on the grounds at night were workers, and they all had keys. Kit squinted at a storage shed that stood near the fence in one of the back corners of the camel pen. She'd be willing to bet even *that* was kept locked.

Suddenly Kit focused sharply on the tall hedge behind the pen's back fence. Could someone slip through that hedge at night?

DETECTIVE WORK

After the Zoo Guide and his tour group moved on, Kit looked around. No workers or zoo policemen in sight! She hurried down a narrow service path that ran toward the hedge between the camel pen and the elk pen next to it. She could hear traffic puttering by on Vine Street, but the hedge was too thick to see through. It was *very* thick, actually. She didn't think anyone could slide through—

Just then she heard a familiar cranky voice coming from inside the storage shed. Otis!

Kit squeezed between the hedge and the back wall of the shed and crouched down. Immediately she felt ridiculous. She shouldn't feel guilty just for walking down a path!

"So the strike leaders are about to reach a settlement with Stephan," Otis was grousing. "Big deal."

"We won't get much out of it," another man said. "That's for certain sure."

Kit heard the shed door bang open. "There's plenty of money to build big, fancy new exhibit areas for the animals." Otis sounded bitter.

"Barless cages. Natural-looking exhibits. As if those things are more important than paying workers a decent wage . . ." His voice faded. Peeking around the shed, Kit saw Otis and another man walking away down the path, lugging a bale of straw.

As she was about to get to her feet, she noticed a gap in the hedge at ground level. Kit poked her arm through the hole, pressing aside the branches. The space wasn't very big, but a child or a small man might be able to squeeze through. Aha!

Thanks, Otis! Kit said silently. She wouldn't have spotted the hole if she hadn't been down low. Now she knew that no matter how closely Officer Culpepper and his Zoo Police guarded the entrance gate, if someone *really* wanted to sneak onto the zoo grounds, he could.

Kit decided that if the expensive new exhibits were making Otis and his friend so angry, she needed to see them for herself. She still had more questions than answers, but she felt that she was finally making some progress in her detective work. Could Otis be so angry about the money being spent on barless cages that he was trying to make trouble?

At the new exhibit, Kit found Stirling's friend Bob talking to a huge crowd. "We believe the animals are happier in natural-looking exhibits," he said. "Those rocks look real, but they're man-made."

Kit caught her breath when she reached the rail. Two tigers stalked about an open grove below. They had trees for shade, and even a pool to splash in. Kit had never before seen tigers that weren't pacing in iron and concrete cages. It was wonderful!

Kit watched the tigers until it was time to meet Stirling. *I'm glad I'm not the superintendent,* she thought. Mr. Stephan clearly had difficult choices to make. Much as she loved the barless grotto, Kit felt some sympathy for Otis. If he was struggling to pay his bills, it would be hard to watch expensive new zoo exhibits being built.

I think I'm getting closer to my big story! Kit thought. Otis's anger about the new exhibits, striking workers, the monkey house door being left open, Will getting blamed—were all these things connected somehow? With a promise to herself to keep investigating, Kit headed back to the monkey house.

❧

About fifteen people—mostly excited children and mothers wearing pretty summer dresses and hats—gathered near the monkey house's front door for Stirling's tour. Kit trailed along at the back, scribbling in her notebook. But Stirling would have been surprised by her notes:

Monkey house door left open last Sunday night. Will on duty.

Monkey house left open Wednesday night. Will on duty.

If Will locked doors when he left, someone must have come along later and unlocked them again.

Who? Why?

DETECTIVE WORK

Strikers unhappy with wages?
Otis unhappy with zoo improvements?

Kit didn't realize the tour group had stopped until she almost tripped over a little girl staring intently into the baboons' cage. *Stirling deserves your attention,* Kit told herself sternly. She'd organize her notes about the zoo's troubles later.

"Baboons are large monkeys that come from dry regions in Arabia and Africa," Stirling began.

A freckled boy pointed at the largest baboon. "That one must be mean." The baboon had a bright red nose, deep-set eyes, and a scowling mouth.

"Rascal looks fierce," Stirling told the group, "but he's fond of children. He once saw a child being spanked, and he got very upset. Now he throws things out of his cage if he sees a child being treated roughly." The freckled boy laughed and tossed a peanut into the cage.

Mixing information with personal stories about the animals, Stirling was polite but in charge. He managed to make himself heard, even when visitors' excited chatter bounced from the rotunda's domed ceiling and a shrill *whoop-whoop-whoop* echoed from the gibbons' cage. With perfect timing, the group arrived at Susie's cage just as she sat at her table with her trainer for dinner. "This is our last stop," Stirling called. "Susie's keeper will be happy to answer any questions you have about gorillas."

"You did a super job," Kit told her friend as the crowd pressed closer to the safety railing in front of Susie's cage. "I'll write a wonderful article about you."

"It should be mostly about the Zoo Guides program, not me," Stirling protested, picking a stray thread from his shirt. But Kit could tell he was pleased.

"You're done for the day, right?" she asked. Looking over her shoulder to make sure no one was in earshot, she added, "I've got some things to tell you. Come on."

She led Stirling outside and down the slope toward the camel pen. "I don't believe Will is responsible for those unlocked doors," she began. "If someone is trying to break into the monkey house, he might be able to get onto the grounds at night by slipping through that hedge along Vine Street." She pointed. "I checked, and there's a space big enough to crawl through behind that shed. There are probably other spots, too."

Stirling squinted across the camel pen. "I suppose it's possible. But why would someone want to do that?"

"I don't know," Kit admitted. "*Yet*. But listen to this. I also heard Otis and another man complaining about money being spent on the new barless cages. They seemed pretty mad at Superintendent Stephan."

"We should keep our eye on Otis," Stirling agreed. Then he glanced at his watch. "Come on. It's almost five. Let's go find Will."

Most of the zoo's large bird collection flittered and flapped in a row of small buildings linked by large outdoor cages. Keepers let the birds into the outdoor cages during warm weather. Visitors strolling along a shady path could enjoy parakeets, strawberry finches, and brightly colored birds called troupials from the West Indies and South America. Kit and Stirling found Will behind one of the buildings, pushing a wheelbarrow filled with soiled straw.

"Hello, Will," Kit said. "We heard there was more trouble, and we want to help."

Will leaned on a shovel, looking tired. "I *know* that door was secure when I left," he insisted. "I double-checked every door in my area."

Kit stared at a brilliant blue-and-yellow bird in the nearest cage. "What time did you finish your work?" she asked finally.

"I left a little after nine o'clock, just like always." Will sighed. "Officer Culpepper found the door unlocked an hour later."

"It can't be a coincidence," Stirling said. "One door left unlocked—maybe. But twice in one week?"

"I don't know what's going on," Will said, setting the shovel across his wheelbarrow. "But there's nothing I can do about it. I'm just a hobo. Nobody's going to believe me."

The look in his eyes twisted Kit's heart. "We believe you, Will!"

"Thanks. But you're not the ones to decide if I should get fired." He shook his head. "Listen, don't worry about it. I'll see you back at the house later." He picked up the wheelbarrow handles and walked away.

"We've got to do something!" Kit said. *I'm just a hobo,* Will had said—she *hated* that!

"He probably *will* get fired if anything else happens," Stirling said gloomily. "But what can we do?"

A lion roared in the distance, and the first faint notes from an orchestra drifted through the trees. Kit imagined gaily dressed couples settling in for an evening of Zoo Opera, never guessing that a penniless young man named Will was in danger of losing his job. She tried to gather her thoughts and consider the problem not as a friend, but as a reporter.

"All right," she said finally. "I've got a couple of ideas."

6

THE BLACK MARKET

Dad was pouring orange juice into glasses the next morning when Kit came in to help with breakfast. "Good morning, Kit!" he said. He wore his overalls and a cheerful smile, which meant he was heading to his airport job. "What are your plans for the day?"

Kit began pulling serving platters from the cupboard. "After chores, I'm going back to the zoo. I'm going to ask Superintendent Stephan for an interview."

"The zoo again? Have you written the pet show story yet?" asked Dad.

"I've got all weekend to work on that," Kit reminded him. She hadn't forgotten about the pet show story, but it was hard to concentrate on that when she was on the trail of a big news story—one that was somehow affecting Will!

"That's strange." Mother stood staring into the pantry.

"What's that, dear?" Dad asked.

Mother turned to face them. "I was planning to serve peach slices with the cereal. I had three peaches in the pantry yesterday. And now they're gone!"

"Gone?" Kit looked sharply at Mother. *Oh no,* she thought. *Not again!*

"One of the boarders probably helped himself—or herself—to a snack," Dad said.

Mother closed her eyes for a moment, then took a deep breath. "I *must* have control in my own kitchen. It's time I put down a couple of ground rules."

She waited until all the boarders were seated at the table. "I need to make a request," she said in a polite but no-nonsense tone. "Some fruit I planned to serve with our morning meal is missing from the pantry."

Kit glanced around the table. Mrs. Dalrymple frowned. Mr. Peck looked confused. Miss Bravetti looked nervous, but no more than usual. Will stared at his plate, his face closed, as if someone had drawn curtains over his thoughts.

"I'm sure you can all appreciate that I need to keep careful track of food in order to serve large meals on a budget," Mother continued. "So please, if you need a snack, speak with me first."

Kit waited for someone to say, *Oh my goodness, Mrs. Kittredge, I apologize. I meant to ask you about those peaches and it slipped my mind.* But no one spoke.

Stirling nudged Kit beneath the table. Kit guessed what he was thinking. There was no blaming a passing hobo this time. The person who'd taken the peaches was sitting at their table.

❧

"I'll make the sandwiches," Kit offered after breakfast. Stirling and Dad needed to take lunch with them.

Mother set a stack of dirty dishes by the sink. "Use the leftover biscuits. And why don't you see if there are any ripe tomatoes in the garden?"

Kit slipped out the back door, happy to escape washing dishes for at least a little while. She'd taken only a few steps when she heard voices, hushed but urgent.

"But I *saw* you!" That was Miss Bravetti, around the corner of the house. Kit froze.

The second voice was pitched too low for Kit to hear clearly. Straining her ears, Kit recognized Will's drawl, but his voice was so hushed, she could only make out a few words. ". . . afraid . . . secret . . . the Kittredges."

Miss Bravetti's voice dropped to a whisper. Kit started to creep closer to the corner of the house. Suddenly the back door slammed, and she jumped.

"Kit?" Mother called.

"Yes?" Kit felt her face flush, as if Mother might be able to tell she'd been eavesdropping.

"See if any more peas are ready, too. All right?"

"Sure!" Kit smiled brightly and hurried on to the garden. But her stomach churned as she stooped among the tomato plants. What had Miss Bravetti and Will been discussing? Miss Bravetti often seemed nervous when talking about anything other than teaching, but just now, she had sounded downright afraid.

Will suddenly appeared around the corner of the house, walking across the backyard. "Heading out?" Kit called.

"Yep." He waved in her direction but didn't catch her eye or stop to chat. Kit watched as he disappeared into the alley, passing the "kind-hearted woman" sign on the fencepost. His shift at the zoo didn't start until noon. Where was he going so early?

Kit dashed around the house, but the teacher had already disappeared. Kit frowned. *Was* Miss Bravetti afraid of Will? What exactly had she seen? What secret had she discovered?

THE BLACK MARKET

After chores, Kit tucked her notebook and pencil into her book bag and headed for the zoo. As she walked down Vine Street, she rehearsed the questions she wanted to ask Mr. Stephan. A good reporter needed to be prepared!

Then Kit spotted a man sitting on a bench ahead. His elbows rested on his knees, his face in his hands, but she recognized his bright red jacket. The slump in his shoulders suggested such hopelessness that Kit felt sad all the way to her toes. "Excuse me, sir?"

The man lifted his head. His face was thin, and there were dark hollows beneath his eyes. Kit wished she had brought a sandwich of her own so that she could offer it to him, but she had promised Mother she'd be home in time to help with lunch.

"Sir," she said again, "I know a soup kitchen where you can get a good meal."

He spread his hands and said something she didn't understand.

"Food! I will take you!" Kit pointed at the

man's chest, pretended she was spooning soup into her mouth, then pointed down the street.

The man struggled to find English. "I need . . . there," he managed, pointing toward the zoo. "*Yanosh*—in there."

Kit shook her head. "I'm sorry, I don't understand."

"*Yanosh!*" he cried.

"Sir, I don't know what *yanosh* means!" In desperation, she tried to take the man's arm. "I'll take you to a place where you can get help—"

He jerked away. "No, no!" he cried. "No!" Even with his heavy accent, Kit understood that very clearly.

A woman pushing a baby carriage frowned and hurried past. Kit didn't know how to help the man. "I'm sorry," she told him helplessly, and left him alone.

Well, that's a good reminder, she told herself. *I've got more than one thing to talk to Superintendent Stephan about.*

THE BLACK MARKET

The ticket seller at the entrance gate pointed Kit toward the administration building, where a secretary gave her a friendly greeting. "A meeting about the Independence Day celebration is just ending," the secretary said. "I'll catch Mr. Stephan and let him know you're here."

Superintendent Stephan's office was lined by shelves overflowing with books, files, snake skins, two tusks, what looked like a jawbone, dusty photographs of exotic animals, and other interesting clutter that Kit itched to investigate. Before she had time to take more than a quick look around, the superintendent walked into the office and extended a hand. His knuckles were knobbed with age, but his grip was firm and confident. "Sol Stephan," he said simply. "I understand you're a reporter. What can I do for you?" His tone was businesslike, but his eyes crinkled with kindness.

"Well, sir, I just have a few questions." Kit flipped to the page in her notebook where she'd carefully made some notes. "How do you feel the Zoo Guides program is working?"

"I'm very pleased. The boys do an excellent job. Education is an important part of our mission, and the Zoo Guides help our visitors understand what they're seeing. I don't know what we'd do otherwise, with money so tight."

"Is the zoo in financial trouble?" Kit flushed. "I mean, I remember hearing some rumors about the zoo possibly closing—"

"That *will not* happen." The superintendent's voice was firm. "Once, when money got so tight that I couldn't pay salaries, I asked the men to stick with it until I could raise more funds. Almost every one of them did." He waved his hand. "That scare prompted all those stories about the zoo going bankrupt. I got hundreds of letters from people who wanted to buy our animals."

Kit scribbled as fast as she could. "Is it common for people to keep wild animals as pets? I saw two baby alligators on display at a pet show last weekend."

"We get requests all the time from people who want to buy our animals." The superintendent leaned back in his chair and laced his fingers together. "Exotic birds are favorite pets, and the little cats, such as ocelots—we have two in our collection—are a big draw. So are the smaller species of monkey and ape. Babies of all kinds always bring in a flood of letters." He chuckled. "The lads who own those baby alligators you saw will be calling on us in a few months, desperate for help with their *grown* alligators."

"Where would someone even get a baby alligator?" Kit asked.

Mr. Stephan's smile disappeared. "I'm afraid there is quite a black market for wild animals of all kinds."

"Black market?" Kit frowned.

"When I acquire animals for our zoo, I work only with reputable collectors—men who I know will treat animals well and sell at a fair price. But there are many unscrupulous dealers who collect animals in the wild by whatever means they can and sell them to private collectors."

Unscrupulous. Kit locked that word in her memory so that she could look it up later. It was a lovely word that meant, she suspected, something distinctly un-lovely. "Do you think someone might try to steal a zoo animal? For the black market?"

"It's possible," Mr. Stephan admitted. "Wild animals bring a huge price on the black market."

Kit's pencil scratched across the page, then paused as a sickening thought hit her like a punch in the stomach. "Everyone loves the babies," Rudy had once said, and Mr. Stephan had just echoed that thought. Would baby animals be the most valuable of all on the black market?

She forced herself to concentrate. "Here's another question. When I visited on Monday, I passed some strikers carrying picket signs, but I didn't see any today. Does that mean the strike is over?"

"It is," Superintendent Stephan said coolly. "The strike never involved more than a few men. I'm fair to my workers. My first responsibility, however, is to my animals."

Kit closed her notebook, aware that she was

talking with an extremely busy man. "Just one more question, sir. Well, a suggestion." She took a deep breath. "Earlier this week I saw a man being turned away from the gate because he didn't have a quarter. Today I saw him again. I think he's out of work, and hungry, and very, very sad. I thought that maybe you could name a special day when poor people could come to the zoo for free."

The elderly man behind the desk nodded slowly, his eyes narrowed as if he was deep in thought. "Thank you for the suggestion, Miss Kit. I will keep it in mind."

Kit had to be satisfied with that. "Thank you, Mr. Stephan." She shook his hand. "You have been very helpful."

❧

"Gosh! I had to move fast to get back here in time to meet you," said Kit. "Mother wanted me to help wash woodwork after lunch." Kit had found Stirling at their usual spot near the monkey house, and she plopped onto a shaded bench to catch her breath.

"I'm in between tours," Stirling assured her. "Did you interview Superintendent Stephan?"

"I did!" Kit said, feeling a bit triumphant. "I started by asking about the Zoo Guides program—he's very impressed with the Guides, by the way—but I also got some very interesting information that might have something to do with Will's problem." She quickly told Stirling what she'd learned about the strike and about the black market.

Stirling cocked his head thoughtfully. "What do you make of all this?"

"Let's start at the beginning." Kit flipped her notebook open. "We know someone is unlocking the monkey house after hours and letting Will take the blame."

"But *why?*"

"I think we've got a couple of possible reasons. One, someone may be trying to steal animals and sell them. Mr. Stephan mentioned unscrupulous wild animal collectors—that means collectors who don't have any morals. If someone wanted to sell wild animals on the black market, it might be easier to steal them from a zoo than to go to Africa or someplace."

"Sell wild animals?" Stirling wrinkled his nose.

"Mr. Stephan said baby animals are popular." Kit's voice trembled.

Stirling sat up straight. "The baby rhesus monkey!" They exchanged a troubled look. As Kit imagined the baby monkey being pulled from his mother, she clenched her fists.

"But how does the door get unlocked?" asked Stirling.

Kit tapped the notebook with her finger. "Someone who works here, and has a key, must be sneaking back after the late shift ends at nine o'clock."

"Maybe someone who works here is getting paid by an un-scroo-pew-lous animal dealer to leave the door open!" Stirling sounded excited.

"That's what I think, too!" Kit exclaimed. She waited until a little girl with bouncing braids skipped past before continuing. "And maybe the worker with the key is afraid of getting caught actually stealing."

Stirling's face fell. "But if someone who works here wants to steal animals, he could just do it," he pointed out. "Why sneak back, unlock the door, then leave again? And one of the workers' doors inside would also have to be unlocked to let a thief get at the baby or one of the other monkeys."

"If Superintendent Stephan thought the main door was left open simply out of carelessness, he might not have checked inside. Or maybe the thief heard someone coming and ran away before he could actually open one of the cages."

"Maybe."

Kit looked back at her notebook. "That's just one idea. Maybe it's not an unscrupulous dealer at all. The culprit could be a worker who has a grudge against Mr. Stephan. Maybe one of the strikers."

A warm breeze brought them the smell of roasting peanuts and hot dogs from a small, gaily painted refreshment cart parked nearby. "Get your peanuts here!" called a young man cheerfully as he filled little white paper sacks with the steaming nuts. *It's strange to be here talking about trouble,* Kit thought. She wished that everyone at the zoo was as cheerful as the man selling snacks.

"There's one more possibility." Stirling darted a glance at her, then looked away.

"What's that?"

"That Will *is* somehow mixed up in something bad." Stirling's voice was so low, she could hardly hear him. "The problems didn't begin until he started working here. And we know he's desperate for money to pay his mother's doctor bills. Maybe one of those unscrupulous animal dealers offered him money to—"

"No." Kit crossed her arms over her chest. "Not Will."

"But ever since he came back to Cincinnati . . ." said Stirling reluctantly. "Well, it's not just here at the zoo. There's the business with the missing food at home."

"I don't believe it! Why would Will steal from us? The first time he came to our house, he wouldn't even accept a meal until he'd done chores for it."

"That was two years ago," Stirling said. "A lot might have happened to him since then."

Kit thought about the changes she'd noticed herself—the shadows in Will's eyes, the smile that didn't seem quite as broad—but she still didn't believe that he was involved in something bad.

"Do you remember talking with Will that first summer about stealing?" Stirling asked. "He said something about the rules changing when you live on the road."

Kit searched her memory. "He was talking about taking an extra potato or two if a stingy farmer didn't pay him fairly for doing chores," she protested. "I *know* Will isn't involved with anything bad now." But against her wishes, she remembered something else: Will's sober voice saying, "On the road . . . well, sometimes you have to do whatever it takes to survive."

"Who else is likely to have taken the peaches?" Stirling asked. "Mr. Peck's lived with us for two years. Miss Bravetti's so skinny, she couldn't possibly be eating snacks. And if Mrs. Dalrymple wanted something, she'd just say so straight out."

"I don't know what's going on at home," Kit admitted. "But I'm just not ready to think Will's behind it."

Stirling sighed. "Me either, I guess."

Kit didn't think Stirling sounded very sure. "Well, *I'm* going to do something about this trouble at the zoo," she announced. "I'm going to write a news article about everything that's going on."

"What good will that do?"

"If the editor publishes my story in the newspaper, it might make the troublemaker nervous," she explained. "Maybe he'll make a mistake, or even confess!"

"Maybe." Stirling didn't sound very sure about that, either.

"It's a good idea," Kit insisted. "I think

writing this story might help Will. And it also gives me a chance to show Gibb that I can write *real* news stories, too."

"Okay!" Stirling held up his hands in surrender. "Listen, I'd better go. I think people are starting to arrive for my tour. I'll see you later."

Kit watched Stirling walk to the monkey house door and greet the families gathering for the day's last tour. In spite of the heat, he still looked trim and tidy in his Guide uniform. She smiled, remembering the scrawny, overprotected boy she'd met almost three years earlier. People *did* sometimes change, she thought. Then her smile faded. Had Will changed, too?

7
A STRANGER IN THE SHADOWS

"Thank you for breakfast," Will said politely the next morning. He'd caught Kit and Mother in the kitchen as they washed dishes. "I wanted to let you know that I won't be here for lunch or dinner."

Kit frowned. "But . . . isn't Saturday your day off?"

Mother's damp hand settled on Kit's shoulder with a clear message: *Don't ask personal questions.* "Fine, Will," she said. "Thank you for letting me know."

Will avoided Kit's gaze as he left the kitchen, and Kit felt a tiny ache bloom inside her chest. "Mother, do you think Will took the missing food?" The question popped out.

Mother hesitated. "I don't know," she said

finally, reaching for another dirty plate. "He's always seemed to be a nice young man. But we really don't know very much about him, do we?"

I know he's got an honest heart! Kit protested, but only silently. Arguing wouldn't change anything.

Kit's big job on Saturday was laundry, and with eight people living at the Kittredge home, Kit had a mountain of sheets and pillowcases to wash and hang on the line. She also had to feed the chickens, drag rugs outside and beat them free of dust, and pick cucumbers. The temperature simmered into the nineties, and Kit soon felt like a worn-out dishrag.

She tried to think about Will and the unlocked doors and the missing food, but her instincts seemed to dribble away with the sweat rolling down her neck. *Where does Will go?* she wondered, swatting away a mosquito as she knelt among the cucumber vines. He hadn't been paid yet, so he couldn't be doing anything that cost money. With the troubles he'd had at

the zoo, she didn't think he would spend
his free day there. So why had Will taken to
disappearing whenever he wasn't at work?
His only friends were right there at the
boarding house!

As she brushed the tiny spines from a
cucumber, her hand suddenly froze. She was
wrong about that. Will *did* have other friends.
His oldest friends, perhaps his best friends,
were hoboes. If any of the hoboes Will knew
had lingered in Cincinnati, they'd likely be
camped out near Union Station.

And they would be hungry.

❧

When Kit hauled a basket of cucumbers
and tomatoes into the kitchen that afternoon,
the sticky air smelled like vinegar. Mother
was heating a brine mixture for pickling the
cucumbers. Beads of perspiration danced on her
forehead, but the tight line of her mouth made
it clear that more than the heat was aggravating

her. At the table, Mrs. Dalrymple and Miss Bravetti were up to their elbows in flour.

"Work the dough with your hands, Angela," the widow instructed. "If it feels too dry, add a bit of the lemon juice."

"Where shall I put these cukes?" Kit asked Mother.

"Leave them on the porch. I'll tend to them when I have a bit more elbow room." Only someone who knew Mother as well as Kit did would have heard the faint edge in her voice.

Mrs. Dalrymple smiled. "I'll have these buns in to bake in no time, Mrs. Kittredge, and we'll all enjoy some extra treats this evening." She gave a self-satisfied nod. "No need to thank me."

Kit took one look at Mother's face and quickly escaped. After apologizing to Grace for leaving her alone so much, Kit left the yard and began walking briskly.

A short while later, she saw the enormous marble-and-steel arch of the Union Station building looming ahead. She passed well-dressed people coming and going from the train station, and then she passed the busy train yard. Her steps slowed as she headed toward the river and the hobo camps. Should she ask for Will? Or sneak close and try to spot him?

Kit and Stirling had first visited the hobo "jungle" with Will two years earlier. *Nothing has changed,* Kit thought sadly as she crept toward the dirty tents and ramshackle shelters pitched in a little grove of trees beneath the train trestle. Most of the hoboes were men, but some women and children were in camp, too. *I should have brought food!* she scolded herself silently, and she promised herself she'd come back.

Kit's garden-stained work clothes didn't attract notice. A train thundered across the bridge overhead, then disappeared over the river. Kit smelled wood smoke and heard a low rumble of men's voices. She paused behind a large tree and peeked around the trunk.

Half a dozen men sprawled on the ground or perched on empty crates around a campfire in a clearing ahead. A man with a long beard ladled soup from a big iron kettle. *Hobo stew,* Kit thought. Will had told her that any hobo who contributed some vegetables or a bit of meat to the pot could look forward to a filling meal.

Suddenly Kit caught her breath. Will was crouched on the far side of the fire. The bearded man handed him a big tin cup of stew. Will smiled his thanks—a real smile, the old smile Kit remembered.

Will hadn't asked Mother for any food he could contribute to the hobo stew, yet here he was. Kit closed her eyes and pressed her forehead against the tree's rough bark, wishing she hadn't come.

❧

Clickety clack! Nothing cheered Kit up like the sound of her typewriter keys, and on Sunday afternoon, she finally had time to write. In her attic alcove, sitting in her swivel chair at her rolltop desk, she felt like a real reporter. And writing helped push aside the memory of seeing Will eating contentedly at the hobo camp.

She was making good progress when Stirling found her. "Hey, Kit. Whatcha working on?" He perched on the edge of her bed.

"My story about the troubles at the zoo." Kit paused, wiping sweaty fingers on her skirt.

"Did you tell Will you saw him at the jungle yesterday?" Stirling asked quietly.

"No!" Kit flared, wishing she hadn't told Stirling about her trip to the hobo jungle. "He'd know I was spying on him! And I won't accuse him of stealing without proof!"

"Okay, okay! For Pete's sake, Kit, I was just asking." Stirling shrugged. "How's your story about the pet show coming? Isn't that due tomorrow?"

"I haven't started yet." She noticed Stirling's surprised frown. "I will! But this story about the zoo is important. It has to be just right. I'll do the pet show article tonight. I've got plenty of time."

Stirling shrugged. "I was hoping you'd work

on a jigsaw puzzle with me, but I can see you're too busy."

"Another time," Kit called as her friend headed toward the stairs. She reached for a dictionary, needing to check the spelling of *skulking.* Now *that* was a word to spark the imagination!

Kit worked on the zoo article for the rest of the afternoon. After dinner she polished it again. When it was as crisp and clear as she could make it, she carefully typed a clean copy. Then she got out her notes about the pet show and began writing that story.

The sky beyond Kit's windows had darkened from deep blue to black when Kit heard someone knock at the foot of the attic stairs. "Hello?" Miss Bravetti called. "Kit, may I come up?"

"Sure!"

"I wanted to remind you of my offer to read your article," Miss Bravetti said, coming to stand behind Kit's chair. *"Alligator* has two *l*'s, Kit."

"I was just about to check." Kit patted the

dictionary, then glanced at her clock. "Gosh!
I didn't realize how late it is."

Miss Bravetti covered a yawn with her hand.
"Everyone else has gone to bed, and I really
need to turn in myself. I can check the story for
you tomorrow morning, if you'd like."

"I should probably go ahead and type my
clean copy tonight," Kit said, feeling guilty for
not taking advantage of Miss Bravetti's help.
"Mornings get so busy. I sure appreciate the
offer, though. But Miss Bravetti?"

"Yes?"

Kit hesitated. "I was just wondering . . . is
everything all right? Are you getting along with
the other boarders?"

Miss Bravetti stiffened. "Of course, Kit.
Good night."

Well, that hadn't gotten her anywhere!
As Miss Bravetti disappeared down the stairs,
Kit sighed and turned back to her typewriter.

Thirty minutes later, she stood and stretched.
The room was so hot that she could hardly
breathe, and she went to the window and pushed

aside the limp curtains.

Tomorrow I'll drop off the stories at the newspaper office, she thought, *and then I'll head back to the zoo.* Much as she hated the idea, she wanted to interview Otis. If she asked the right questions, he might just—

A sudden movement in the yard below interrupted her thoughts. Kit saw a figure skulking through the shadows by the chicken coop. *It must be Will, sneaking back to the hobo jungle,* Kit thought, and she felt fresh disappointment slide down to her toes.

As she watched, the figure emerged from the shadows and hurried across a moonlit patch of lawn to the gate. Kit saw his silhouette clearly. He wore a brimmed hat—the kind Dad called a fedora.

Will didn't own a fedora. He wore a tattered cap with a bill that shaded only his forehead.

The perspiration on Kit's skin suddenly felt cold. If the man sneaking through her backyard wasn't Will, who was he?

Kit quickly padded down the stairs. She

needed to wake her parents! But as she reached the landing, her feet slowed. Surely the man was already gone; it was too late for Dad to catch him. Grace was inside, and so were all of the boarders—except Will, who slept on the back porch.

Suppose Mother and Dad decided the skulker must be a friend of Will's? Even without proof that Will was doing bad things, they might tell him to leave! And if jumpy Miss Bravetti heard there was a stranger skulking about the house, she might move out, too!

Kit stood shivering in the shadows for a few moments longer, uncertain. Finally, she went back up to the attic and tried to sleep, but her brain was too full of questions and her heart too full of worry.

8
SECRETS

The next morning, Dad poked his head into the kitchen while Kit and Mother were preparing breakfast. "Did you take my blue suit, dear?" he asked Mother.

"Your suits have been hanging in the front hall closet for months," Mother told him. "I moved them down so we'd have more room in our closet upstairs."

Dad shook his head. "No, I knew you'd moved them downstairs. But I just noticed that the blue one isn't in the hall closet."

"It must be! Let me go look." Mother wiped her hands on a towel and hurried from the room. A moment later she returned, frowning. "I can't find it either. I can't imagine what happened to it."

Kit and Mother exchanged a troubled look. Then Kit busied herself with the silverware. She didn't know anything about Dad's best suit, but she *did* know that Will was keeping secrets. She *did* know that a stranger had crept across their backyard the night before.

"I still have my old gray one," Dad was saying. "It's a bit threadbare, but it's not as if I need to wear it every day."

"But you'll need your good suit for job interviews one day!" Kit protested. "When the Depression is over."

He looked ruefully down at his rough work clothes. "I liked selling cars, but now I'm learning about airplanes. Things change." He squeezed her shoulder. "Don't worry, Kit. Things will work out somehow."

Kit sat down to breakfast with a lump of worry in her chest. Fortunately, Mrs. Dalrymple took charge of the conversation. "Everyone must try one of Angela's cinnamon rolls," she ordered, "and one of my *kifli*."

"What are *kifli*, Mrs. Dalrymple?" Stirling

asked, taking a roll and one of the small, crescent-shaped pastries.

"They're pastries filled with jam. Mine are particularly light, I must say. The recipe came from my mother, who was born in Hungary." For an instant Kit thought she saw sadness in Mrs. Dalrymple's eyes. Then it was gone. "Kit, did I hear you say you're walking downtown today?" she asked. "You can take whatever *kifli* and rolls are left over to the soup kitchen. I can always make more."

"Be glad to," Kit said. "I'm going to deliver my first assignment to the newspaper office."

"If you don't mind, I'll take a couple of your pastries with me to orchestra practice," Mr. Peck told Mrs. Dalrymple. "We're having long rehearsals to prepare for the Fourth of July concert at the zoo this Thursday. Just three more days!"

Stirling sat up straight. "It's going to be a great celebration! I can't wait!"

"What fun!" Dad said. "I think we all should go to the zoo that evening."

SECRETS

"I can pack a picnic supper," Mother offered.

Mrs. Dalrymple nodded. "Excellent idea."

Kit glanced around the table. Miss Bravetti hadn't said a word, and Kit wondered if the zoo's admission price troubled the young schoolteacher, or if she was simply getting tired of having Mrs. Dalrymple making decisions for her. Will's expression was a polite blank, and Kit's stomach twisted back into a knot. *Will,* she thought, *what are you thinking?*

❧

The newspaper office hummed with that sense of urgency Kit found so exciting. Gibb sat at his desk, rattling away on his typewriter. He barely paused as Kit approached his desk. "Is that your story?" he barked. "Just leave it." Kit gave the envelope containing *both* her stories a pinch for luck, then dropped it into the "IN" basket on the desk.

When she stood on the street again, she drew a deep breath and blew it out. *That* was done. Now she'd just have to wait and see what Gibb thought of her zoo story.

After dropping off the pastries at the soup kitchen, Kit walked on toward the zoo. She found the same unhappy man on Vine Street. He paced on the sidewalk, muttering.

"Excuse me, sir?" Kit reached into her book bag and pulled out a small sack. With Mother's blessing, Kit had packed an extra lunch that morning, just in case she ran across the red-jacketed man again.

He accepted the bag and cautiously pulled out the hearty ham and cheese sandwich, wrapped in waxed paper. The distress in his eyes faded. He said something in his own language, but his meaning was clear.

"You're welcome," Kit said. "I wish I could do more."

He slid the sandwich into one of the big pockets in his red jacket, then glanced back into the sack. His expression slowly changed to one of wonder. *"Kifli?"*

"Why . . . yes!" Kit grinned. *"Kifli!"*

110

He stared at the pastry for a moment, then lifted it out and ate it very slowly. His eyes cleared, and a smile creased his face. He reached for Kit's hand and pumped it gratefully.

"You're welcome!" Kit said again. When she headed on toward the zoo, her steps had an extra bounce.

❧

She found Stirling at the monkey house, busy with a tour. She waved, then wandered around the exhibits to occupy herself until her friend was free. She hoped he could tell her where Otis might be.

I've spent so much time here, I could give tours myself, she thought. Rascal the baboon's colorful glare didn't seem quite so threatening today, and Kit smiled, wondering if he'd been forced to defend any roughly handled children lately. She could recognize several of the chimpanzees by name now. Buddy Boy still liked to sit quietly by himself, while two scamps named Kip and

Jester constantly delighted visitors by tumbling about the cage.

"Hey, Kit!" Rudy stood at her elbow. "You should get a job here!"

Kit laughed. "If I weren't working on my newspaper career, I might."

Rudy put down a bucket heavy with fruit and absently rubbed the crease in his palm. "You still working on a story about the zoo?"

"Um . . . yes, I am!" Kit nodded briskly, hoping she wouldn't have to go into too many details. "I'd like to interview you sometime. And I want to see if Otis will give me an interview."

"Otis!" Rudy looked startled. "Why Otis?"

"I thought that maybe if I ask him nicely, it might put him in a good mood. You know, make him feel important."

Rudy sighed. "Maybe it would have, but you're too late. Otis got fired this morning."

"*Fired!*" Kit exclaimed, then quickly lowered her voice. "Why did he get fired?"

Rudy shook his head. "Otis came to work

this morning with his hand bandaged up, claiming he'd been bitten. The superintendent said Otis must have mishandled the animal."

Suddenly Kit had a terrible thought. She grabbed Rudy's arm. "Rudy, have you seen the baby rhesus monkey today?"

He frowned. "No. Why?"

"Can we take a look? Right now?"

"Well . . . I'm supposed to be feeding the orangutans, but that can wait a minute, I guess." Rudy picked up his bucket and led the way to the veterinary room.

Kit scanned the room quickly and blew out a long breath when she saw mama and baby safe and sound. "I was afraid Otis had stolen the baby to sell on the black market."

"The black market!" Rudy looked shocked. "Why did you think that?"

"It was just an idea I had." Kit stared into the cage. Her heart melted all over again at the sight of the defenseless baby. His black eyes met hers, curious but not afraid. Kit didn't want him to *ever* learn to be afraid of humans.

"I thought maybe the mother monkey bit Otis when he tried to take her baby."

Rudy shrugged. "For whatever it's worth, Otis said a chimp bit him."

I don't think that's worth much, Kit thought as they went back to the main hall. If Otis *had* been trying to steal the baby rhesus monkey, lying about his injury wouldn't have troubled his conscience at all!

❧

After some searching, Kit found Will in a storage shed behind the aviaries, breaking open a bale of straw. The shed smelled musty and sweet, like freshly cut grass. "Hello, Will," she said, trying to sound cheerful. "I brought you a snack. Can you take a break?"

"Well . . . okay. Thanks." He wiped his hands on his pants. "But no more than a minute, Kit. I'm in enough trouble as it is."

Kit pulled the last parcel from her book bag. "Here. Compliments of the mighty

Mrs. Dalrymple." She handed him a roll.

"She's not so bad," Will said unexpectedly. "I bet she's kept busy all of her life. Now she doesn't have a home or family of her own, and she doesn't know what to do with herself." He stared at the cinnamon roll, then looked at Kit. "Do you have something else on your mind?"

"Well, it feels like we hardly ever see you, Will." Kit's face grew warm. "It's just that—"

"It's just that ever since I came back to Cincinnati, there's been nothing but trouble." Will looked her straight in the eye. "I haven't done anything wrong, Kit."

"I believe you." Kit's voice was firm, and she realized—with a touch of relief—that even now, she did.

"Something funny is going on at the zoo," Will said, his voice low. "I've noticed a few things myself. Little things, like a bucket gone missing from the monkey house, and a burlap sack of clean straw I'd set aside—"

"That proves you're not to blame!" Kit cried. "Did you tell your boss?"

He shook his head. "It doesn't prove a thing. Look, Kit, I know how the world works. Nobody will take a hobo's word for *anything*. I have to hang on here until Saturday—that's payday. But unless I can find a way to prove I'm not to blame, I'll be hitting the rails again as soon as I get paid."

Saturday! Time was running out. Kit took a deep breath. "There's something else. Looking out my window last night, I saw a man wearing a fedora sneak through our backyard. Since you sleep on the back porch, I wondered if you saw him too." She looked at her friend intently, longing to see surprise in his face.

Instead he looked at his rough work boots and hitched one shoulder in a little shrug.

"Did you see him?" Kit pressed. "Is he someone you know?"

"Sorry," he said lightly. "I wish I could help you." It *sounded* as if he didn't know anything, but Kit couldn't help noticing his careful choice of words. Will knew more than he was willing to reveal.

9
PLANNING A STAKEOUT

So much for my detective work, Kit thought as Will went back to work. An eagle's cry shrilled from the flight cage. A little girl skipped past, clutching her mother's skirt with one hand and a green balloon with the other. Kit hardly noticed, instead thinking hard about her crumbling investigation. Otis was gone, Rudy and Stirling were busy, and Will was keeping secrets.

She didn't know what else she could accomplish at the zoo that afternoon, so she headed to the gate and turned toward the newspaper office. She was itching to get Gibb's reaction to her zoo article.

Gibb was at his desk, talking with the lady reporter. "You did a good job, Jones," he was saying. "I'm running your story on page one—*above* the fold."

"Thanks, Gibb!" As Miss Jones turned away, she smiled at Kit. "Nice to see you, Kit."

Gibb's greeting wasn't nearly as warm. "Sit down, Kit. We need to have a talk."

Looking at the editor's face, Kit felt a cold lump grow in her chest. She slid into the chair. "Yes, sir?" she asked finally.

Gibb dropped a piece of paper into Kit's lap. "What is this?"

Kit stared at the typed words she'd worked so hard on. "It's . . . it's a story about trouble at the Zoological Garden," she said in a small voice. "Everyone in Cincinnati loves the zoo, so I thought . . . I thought it would make a good subject for a news story."

"Your assignment wasn't a news story," said Gibb. "I asked you to write a fun children's piece. That's all."

Kit rubbed her palms on her skirt. "I *did* write the pet show story, too."

"Yes. The pet show story." Gibb dropped

Kit's second article into her lap. "Compared to the zoo story, how much time did you spend on this piece?"

Kit swallowed hard. "Well . . . not very much," she admitted.

"And it shows. This isn't up to our standards, Kit. It isn't up to *your* standards. I'm disappointed in you."

Tears stung Kit's eyes, and she fiercely blinked them back. The ache in her chest grew bigger. "I'm very sorry, Mr. Gibson," she said slowly. "I let you down. I thought I was doing something good, but . . . but I can see that I made a big mistake."

Gibb's expression softened—just a bit. "Well, at least you're taking responsibility for your mistake. If you didn't do that, I'd toss you out by the ear. *All* reporters make mistakes sometimes. You have to admit them and then try to make things as right as you can."

Kit sat up straighter. "If you're willing to give me a second chance, I'll turn in the best children's story you ever saw."

Gibb considered, tapping his fingers on the desk. "All right. We'll give it another shot." He looked again at Kit's story. "The pet show is old news now, so you'll need to find something else. Have it here a week from today. That's Monday, July eighth."

"I can do that," Kit promised as she tucked the story back into her book bag. "I really, really, *really* appreciate getting the second chance."

"You're welcome." Gibb squinted at her, toying with a pencil. "And Kit. About the other piece."

"Yes?" Kit held her breath.

"I don't think you were ready to write that story. My instincts tell me you could find more information if you dug a little deeper. Sometimes reporters have to sit on a good story until it's ready to publish."

Kit knew he was telling her something important. She struggled to understand. "But . . . how can you tell when it's time?"

Gibb shook his head. "I can't give you a

simple answer, Kit. But when you're *really* ready to write that story, I think you'll know."

❧

When she got home, Kit found Mrs. Dalrymple's quilting friends crowding the living room. Mother had retreated to the back porch with the newspaper, but she looked up as Kit approached. "Hello, dear—why, Kit! What's the matter?"

"Gibb didn't buy my pet show story," Kit blurted out. "Oh, Mother, I'm sorry! I tried to impress Gibb by writing a news story about all the troubles at the zoo. I *meant* to do a good job on the pet show story, I really did! But I got so excited thinking about writing a *real* news story that I waited until the last minute." She stared at her shoes.

"Oh, dear."

"I'm sorry," Kit said again. "I promised you I'd get paid a dollar for one story this week, and I'd hoped I could surprise you with *two* dollars. Instead, I didn't earn anything."

"I don't think that's true, Kit," Mother said softly. "It sounds to me like you earned some good experience."

"Experience won't buy groceries," Kit began, but just then Mrs. Dalrymple poked her head out the door.

"I'm sorry to interrupt," she said, not sounding at all apologetic. "Mrs. Kittredge, you did promise me that flour sack with the tiny roses. By chance is it ready?"

"I just used the last of the flour this morning," Mother said. "You'll get the flour sack as soon as it's been washed, Mrs. Dalrymple."

"That will do nicely," the widow announced, and she went back to her friends.

Mother took a deep breath before turning back to Kit. "Are you looking for a new story idea? Are you going to try again?"

Kit nodded. "The pet show is old news already, and I don't want to remind Gibb of my mistake by turning in another zoo story, so my article about the Zoo Guides will have to wait a few weeks."

Mother riffled through the newspaper, then pointed at the Events page. "There's a notice here about a brother-and-sister circus act."

"'See the Flying Zambinis at the Cole Brothers Circus,'" Kit read. "'The trapeze artists, fifteen-year-old twins, are sure to thrill young and old alike.' That's a great idea! Thanks, Mother."

Surely I can write a good article about the Flying Zambinis, Kit thought as she and Mother went to the kitchen to start dinner. *Maybe I should just forget my idea of writing the news story.*

Then she stiffened her backbone. No. She intended to do a *fantastic* job on the circus story. But give up trying to figure out what was happening at the zoo? Give up her *real* dream of reporting news stories? Not a chance!

❧

Miss Bravetti volunteered to help with

kitchen cleanup after supper. Kit told her what had happened at the newspaper office as they washed and dried the dishes. "I shouldn't have left the pet show story for the last minute." Her cheeks grew warm as she remembered her conversation with Gibb. "You were kind enough to offer your help, and I didn't take it."

"I'll tell you what," said Miss Bravetti as she dried her hands on a towel. "If you fetch the story, I'll take a look at it now. Maybe there's something you can learn from it that will help you with the circus story."

They sat together at the kitchen table to review the pet show story. Mother had gone out to the garden, and Kit couldn't help noticing that Miss Bravetti looked more relaxed when the two of them were alone. *She's pretty when she's not worrying about things,* Kit thought as she watched Miss Bravetti read the story. If Kit ever found out what Will had done to frighten the young teacher, she would give him a real scolding!

"You've got some good material here, Kit,"

Miss Bravetti told her. "But I'd like you to think about a more interesting first sentence, something that grabs readers right away."

As they talked, Kit recognized several weak words and sentences. Miss Bravetti also made a few suggestions about organizing a newspaper story. "You want people to keep reading," she said. "Craft every paragraph so that it pulls your reader more deeply into the story."

"I'll do better with the circus piece," Kit said. "Thank you, Miss Bravetti!" She suddenly got a new idea. "Stirling and I are going to work on a jigsaw puzzle this evening," she told her. "You'd be welcome to join us."

"Thank you, Kit, but no," Miss Bravetti said. "I want to take a walk before it gets dark. Come to me when you have a draft of your circus story, though. We'll go over it together."

Kit joined Stirling in the living room, where the jigsaw puzzle was set up on a card table in the corner. They'd both been so busy that very little of the scene—a German castle overlooking a lake—had emerged from the pieces. While

Kit sorted out sky-colored pieces on her side of the table, she told Stirling about her day.

"You'll do a super job on the circus story," Stirling said loyally.

"Thanks." Kit shrugged, still embarrassed by her mistakes. "I'm not giving up on trying to clear Will's name at the zoo, though," she whispered. "If this mystery doesn't get solved by Saturday, Will's going to collect his pay and leave!"

Stirling fitted two edge pieces together. "I had a chance to ask Officer Culpepper a few questions this afternoon, as you suggested. If he has new ideas, he didn't tell me." He looked away for a moment. "You know, Kit, Otis is gone, and I'm sure he had to turn in his keys before he left. There may not be any more trouble."

Kit shook her head. "My instincts tell me that this isn't over. Whoever was trying to sneak into those buildings didn't get whatever he was after. It would be just horrible if that baby monkey disappeared! I think there's still more we need to discover about the zoo troubles." She tried to fit a piece of sky into the puzzle, then slapped it back on the table in frustration. Her thoughts felt like puzzle pieces—scattered bits of information that refused to fit together.

"So, what do you want to do now?" Stirling asked.

"Let's go over what happened again," Kit said. "The door was unlocked last Sunday, and Superintendent Stephan found it. The door was unlocked again last Wednesday, and Officer Culpepper found it. Do you know what Officer Culpepper's schedule is?"

"He's off duty on Sundays and Mondays."

Kit twiddled a puzzle piece in her fingers. "If I was trying to steal a zoo baby for the black market, I'd try on a night when the chief Zoo Police officer is off duty, which is probably why the first attempt happened on a Sunday night."

Stirling nodded. "But Superintendent Stephan is so watchful when Officer Culpepper is off duty that he found the unlocked door anyway."

"So, maybe the thief figured he'd try again when Officer Culpepper *was* on duty. And that failed, too." Kit stared at her friend. "What can the thief try next?"

"I don't know. Maybe . . . maybe create some kind of distraction?"

"Hey!" Kit smacked her palm on the table, scattering puzzle pieces. "Suppose the thief doesn't have to create a distraction? Suppose the zoo helps out by creating a distraction *for* him?"

Stirling looked confused. "Like what?"

"Like a big, noisy, after-dark party!"

"Oh!" Stirling stared at her, his eyes wide. "The Fourth of July celebration!"

Kit was so excited, her words tumbled out. "Think about it, Stirling! The zoo expects huge crowds on Thursday night. Everyone will be near the concert pavilion. And when the sun goes down, fireworks will start booming. If someone still wants to break into the monkey house, it will be the perfect time!"

Stirling leaned closer. "And surely Superintendent Stephan and Officer Culpepper will *both* be busy just keeping an eye on the events and the crowd. If there are other officers on duty that night, they'll be spread thin."

"So *we're* going to fill in," Kit finished triumphantly. Her voice had risen, so she glanced over her shoulder to make sure they were still alone. "Mother and Dad are taking us to the celebration. We can slip away just before dark and go keep an eye on the monkey house."

"How are we going to just 'slip away' from your parents?" Stirling asked.

Kit waved that worry aside. "It shouldn't be too hard. We can offer to take Will some supper."

"I suppose we could do that." Stirling's voice held some doubt. "But, Kit . . . remember, we don't know that anything's going to happen."

"It's the best guess we've got," Kit countered. "We have to do *something* before Saturday, when Will gets paid. Agreed?"

Stirling hesitated for just a moment before

nodding firmly. "Agreed."

Kit felt much better with a plan of action in mind. Maybe nothing would happen Thursday night . . . but her instincts told her that something would.

❦

The next afternoon, Kit packed her notebook and a newly sharpened pencil into her book bag. She was excited about the stakeout plan, but the Fourth of July celebration was still two days away! She wanted to fill the time by working on her assignment from Gibb. She wasn't going to make the same mistake twice!

At the vacant lot at Fourth and Smith streets, crowds of people had already gathered to watch sweating workmen unload equipment from a string of gaudy circus wagons. Other burly men were raising the huge circus tent, and Kit was thrilled to see several elephants pulling the huge support poles upright. Circus performers in sparkling costumes strolled the grounds. *Tootle, tootle, toot!* Kit grinned as a blue-and-gold steam calliope began puffing out a jaunty tune.

A man wearing a gold jacket and top hat stood on a small platform. "Our performances are jam-packed with breathtaking feats!" he promised the crowd. He pointed at several children. "You youngsters will want to see the Flying Zambinis! Just fifteen years old and already the world's finest aerial acrobats!" He waved his arm. "Seats will go fast! Luckily, advance tickets are available at that small red tent!"

As most of the listeners tramped to the red tent, Kit approached the barker. The man lit a cigar while she explained what she hoped to do. "Sure, kid," he said. The cigar clamped between his teeth wiggled as he talked. "You can have an interview with the Flying Zambinis. But come back tomorrow, okay? We're just too busy getting set up right now." He spotted some newcomers and turned away. "Hey, folks, step right up! Let me tell you about the circus!"

Kit sighed impatiently as she walked away. She had wanted to start her new children's story right away! *Well, I guess that means I can investigate the zoo mystery for the rest of the afternoon without feeling guilty,* she thought.

But how? What angle had she missed?

She thought back to her first conversation with Miss Bravetti. The teacher had stressed the importance of research. "Reporters have to interview people," she'd said, "or go to the library to look up information."

What sort of information could she look up? Surely any business records were kept at the zoo, not the public library. No, wait! She'd overlooked one of the *best* sources of information—newspapers!

She headed to the big public library downtown with fresh determination. The four-story stone building on Vine Street was one of her favorite places in Cincinnati. Librarians displayed newly purchased titles on a shelf in the front lobby, and usually Kit stopped to explore those. She loved the faint leathery smell of the bindings and the smooth feel of clean pages just as much as the stories inside! Today, though, she forced herself not to linger by the tempting display and went instead to the reference desk.

"May I help you?" asked the librarian behind the desk. She had neatly bobbed hair and a kind smile.

"Do you keep copies of old newspapers?" Kit asked. "I'd like to look at all the newspapers from the past few weeks."

"I can help you with that," the librarian said. She disappeared into a little room behind the desk. Kit settled down at an empty table, and a few moments later the librarian put a pile of newspapers down beside her.

Kit spent the next two hours searching through each of the newspapers, page by page. She found articles about the zoo workers' strike and about the completion of the new barless animal exhibits that Otis was so angry about. She also found notices about new exotic birds going on display and a photo of the baby rhesus monkey. She jotted down the title of each article, and the date it was published, in her notebook. *This is helpful,* she thought. *Any unscrupulous dealers reading the newspaper would learn about new birds and animals they might want for the black market.*

Kit was pleased to find a feature article about Maria and Marcus Zambini, too.

These aerial acrobats started their careers at age eight with the Clyde and Davis Circus, which was unable to survive the Depression and disbanded a month ago. The Cole Brothers were lucky to hire these rising stars for their show. Their aerial acrobatics will enchant young and old.

Kit realized how helpful it was going to be to have this background information before she interviewed the Zambinis. The more she could learn in advance—

Wait a minute!

Kit stared at the newspaper, her mind

suddenly racing. For a long moment she was completely unaware of the other library visitors passing her table or the annoying flicker of a nearby lamp. Finally she nodded, turned to a clean page in her notebook, and scribbled down a new idea.

I just might make a good reporter after all! she thought. She knew she could do a great job on the children's story before her Monday deadline.

And by then maybe, just maybe, she'd have a big news story to write as well.

10
DANGER AT THE MONKEY HOUSE

As the sun was setting on the Fourth of July, Kit and Stirling hurried away from the zoo's concert pavilion and crowds of picnicking families. Music from the huge merry-go-round competed cheerfully with the orchestra's fine concert piece. Kit impatiently dodged laughing couples and shrieking children who zigzagged back and forth waving flags and eating puffy swirls of cotton candy.

"Phew!" she exclaimed when she and Stirling had left the crush of people behind. "I've felt like a balloon ready to pop all day!"

"Me, too," Stirling confessed.

The day had passed like molasses. Will disappeared right after breakfast, politely declining Dad's invitation to join the family in a game of croquet. In the late afternoon the Kittredges, Mrs. Dalrymple, and Miss Bravetti walked to the zoo in time to catch Stirling's last tour of the day. When the animal houses closed at five o'clock, they ate fried chicken and lemon pound cake while listening to a children's choir. Then came a gymnastics performance by a group of local German-American men and, finally, the concert by Mr. Peck's orchestra.

Escaping from her parents had been easier than Kit had even dared to hope. "For heaven's sake," Mother had whispered to Kit and Stirling when the orchestra paused after a rousing patriotic march. "You're both as jumpy as jackrabbits! Go work off some steam." They hadn't needed a second invitation.

"So, we're really going to go through with this?" Stirling asked now, as they headed toward the monkey house.

"Do you want to back out?"

Stirling took a deep breath. "No. It's our last chance to help Will."

Although electric lights on tall poles lit the intersections of the paths that wove through the grounds, none were placed near outdoor cages, where they would disturb the animals. As Kit and Stirling walked through the shadows, Kit lowered her voice. "All we have to do is follow our plan," she said. "You hide in the bushes near the camel pen and keep an eye out for someone sneaking through the hedge. I hide behind the refreshment cart that's parked near the main entrance of the monkey house. If either one of us sees someone, we go find Officer Culpepper."

"The fireworks start at nine-thirty," Stirling muttered, going over their plan one last time. "If we haven't spotted anyone by the time the fireworks end at ten o'clock, we head back and catch up with your parents."

"Right," Kit whispered. The monkey house loomed silent before them. Even the big outdoor cages were still. "Well, good luck."

As Kit watched Stirling disappear into the shadows, she suddenly felt a nervous shiver.

The music had faded to a distant tinkle. The night air was hot and breathless.

Get moving, Kit! she ordered herself briskly. She hurried over to the refreshment cart and crouched behind it. By peeking around the corner, she could clearly see the main entrance of the monkey house. Her blood seemed to tingle. She was *really* doing detective work now!

The gloom deepened into full night. Soon Kit could no longer make out the shapes of tree trunks nearby. Her knees began to ache, and she eased to an un-detective-like position on the ground, sitting cross-legged. A single lamp cast only a small yellow pool of light near the monkey house. Beyond that glow, strange shadows stretched into blackness. The lawns and gardens around the monkey house, so familiar by day, suddenly seemed spooky and threatening. Just a short walk away, the zoo's concert and picnic grounds were jammed with people, but Kit felt very alone. She wondered how Stirling was doing, crouched by his own lonely self—

Ka-boom!

Kit almost jumped from her skin. The night sky popped with a brilliant cascade of green and yellow sparks. A lion roared in the distance, and a faint "Ahhh!" echoed from the crowd. Kit tried to will her heartbeat back to normal.

Ka-boom! Another thrilling burst of fireworks exploded above her head. Kit stared at the dazzling, dancing fire in the night sky. For a few seconds—just a few!—she forgot her task.

Then a flurry of movement caught her eye. Someone had just crossed through the pool of lamplight! A shadow moved on the steps to the monkey house door. It melted into the building and was gone.

Kit stared at the doorway in disbelief. She'd *missed* him! She'd bungled her chance to identify or describe the troublemaker!

She *had* to see what was going on. Jumping to her feet, she ran lightly across the path and tiptoed up the steps. The door was ajar, and she peeked inside. A single small bulb was mounted above the entrance, but the main hall was bathed in shadows. Kit saw a moving beam of light ahead of her, as if the skulker had turned on a flashlight. It played down the floor toward the building's circular rotunda, paused for a moment on the far side, then disappeared—right by the *Workers Only!* door in the back wall.

So a thief *was* after the baby rhesus monkey! Anger steamed away Kit's fear. No one was stealing that baby if she could help it!

Kit scurried toward the closest wide marble column that marked the edge of the rotunda and pressed herself behind it. The hall, usually ringing with laughter and voices and monkey calls, was spookily quiet. Even the fireworks sounded distant and hushed. Kit's heart was thumping. Despite the heat, her skin felt clammy. *Calm down and think!* she told herself, and took a deep, slow breath. As her eyes adjusted to the gloom, she could just make out the big cages that lined the walls.

Then, from behind the *Workers Only!* door,

she heard a muffled snatch of conversation. *Two* men? Her mouth went dry.

Suddenly, another faint sound from the right caught her ear. Someone was unlocking the *side* door! She heard the door click open, then shut softly again. The bottom of Kit's stomach seemed to plunge toward her knees. Holding her breath, she slid her cheek along the cool marble and peered around the column. The new intruder clicked on a flashlight, and she got a glimpse of his face.

Will.

Kit stood frozen behind the column. She wanted to cry.

Slowly, Will played his flashlight over Susie the gorilla's cage. The light lingered on the doors, then slid silently toward the baboons' cage, which he inspected with equal care.

Will hadn't come to steal anything! He was checking all the cages, making sure for himself that nothing was amiss. Kit almost whooped with relief, but a new thought made her shiver. The monkey thieves were sure to reappear any moment. What would happen if they saw Will? Would he get hurt?

She had to warn him—somehow—without making a sound or startling him from his own silence. And she had only seconds to do it.

Kit watched Will slide silently past the baboons' cage and turn into the narrow hallway in the northeast corner of the building. It led, she remembered, to the spider monkeys' outdoor cage. As he disappeared, Kit took a last glance toward the still-closed *Workers Only!* door, hoping mama monkey was putting up a good fight. Then she darted to the baboons' cage and ducked under the safety bar. Trusting that Rascal truly *was* fond of children, she snatched a piece of chalk from the blackboard by his cage.

She heard Will rattle a lock on the door to the outside cage as she knelt on the floor. Her fingers trembled as she chalked a solid dot on the cement and drew a rectangle around it. Then she scurried back to her hiding place. With sweaty palms pressed against the marble

column, she watched the glow of Will's flashlight appear again. Would her chalk marks
show up on the cement floor?

Will's light stopped moving. Then the
flashlight went out.

Kit felt a flush of triumph. He'd understood
her message! And just in time, because she
heard the *Workers Only!* door open. The glow
of another flashlight appeared. Kit caught the
glint of a large metal pail. The thieves must
have put the baby monkey in the pail.

Suddenly Will's shout rang out: "Hey, you—
stop right there!"

"Be careful, Will!" Kit yelled. The big pail
sailed through the air toward her friend.
"No!" she screamed. The baby monkey would
be hurt!

Kit launched forward. The overhead lights
in the rotunda flared on, their sudden glare
blinding her. Kit's foot landed on something
slippery. She skidded, windmilled her arms,
and landed hard on the floor. The sudden
commotion triggered a deafening chorus of

shrieks, chitters, and roars as the monkeys and apes woke in alarm. Kit smelled bananas. Footsteps pounded past.

Then a huge hand closed around Kit's arm and yanked her to her feet. "What's all this about?" Officer Culpepper growled. A few feet away, another Zoo Police officer held Will.

"They're getting away!" Kit cried. Over Officer Culpepper's shoulder, she caught a glimpse of a man running toward the main entrance. "It's not us! Don't you understand?" When the officer's grip only tightened, she struggled desperately to break free. "Let me go! *The thieves are getting away!*"

11
A REUNION

Just like that, Kit felt Officer Culpepper's fingers release her arm. She raced down the hall after the thieves, shoved the door open, and pounded down the steps.

Ka-boom! In the brief flare, Kit glimpsed two running figures ahead. They were getting away! She pumped her arms, straining for more speed. One man stumbled. She threw herself at him. *Oomph!* Kit felt the breath knocked out of her as they both crashed down on the gravel path. Kit could hardly breathe and her scraped elbows stung, but she held on tight to the man's waist.

Kit knew the second thief was getting away, but as she lifted her head, someone else raced from the shadows and made a flying tackle.

"I got him!" Stirling hollered as he and the other culprit tumbled into a clump of lilies. Stirling had arrived just in time!

The two zoo policemen barreled out the door with Will on their heels. Kit's thief had stopped struggling and lay quietly. Kit got to her feet. "This man was trying to steal the baby rhesus monkey!" she panted. "We need to go back inside and find the baby!"

Officer Culpepper hauled the skulker to his feet and pulled him to the pool of light beneath the lamp by the main entrance. When Kit got her first good look at the thief, she gasped in surprise. It was the red-coated man who liked *kifli!*

"I've always known this no-good lout was trouble," Officer Culpepper said grimly.

"It's not what you think," said someone behind them.

Kit whirled. *"Rudy!"* She stared, shocked, as Stirling and Rudy joined them. The man in the red coat began to weep. Another burst of fireworks seared the sky over their heads, and Kit heard a faint cheer from the crowd.

"It's not what you think," Rudy said again. "Mr. Barta and I weren't after the baby. We were trying to take Buddy Boy, but not for the black market! Buddy Boy's real name is János." Kit recognized the name—it sounded like *yanosh*—as the word Mr. Barta had repeated so desperately the day she'd tried to take him to a soup kitchen.

"But Rudy, *why?*" she demanded.

"Because he belongs to Mr. Barta." Rudy pointed at the man in the red jacket.

"János—belong to me," Mr. Barta said in his labored English, before adding something else in his own language.

Suddenly, a puzzle piece clicked into place in Kit's mind. "Mr. Barta was the monkey trainer for the Clyde and Davis Circus before it went bankrupt! I read about him at the library. I was afraid the circus animals might have been sold on the black market. I wondered if there might be a connection—if maybe a black market dealer targeting the monkey house here might be involved with circus animals, too."

"Clyde and Davis sold their animals," Rudy told them. "I don't know where. But János didn't belong to the circus, and he shouldn't have been sold. Mr. Barta raised him from a baby."

Officer Culpepper didn't look convinced. "We'll have to see records that prove that, son," he said. "Wild animals are too valuable to take the word of some bum."

"He's not a bum!" Kit said fiercely. "He's just poor, and he can't speak English very well. Rudy, can you talk with him?"

Rudy shook his head. "Just a little. Otis told me—"

"Otis!" Will exclaimed.

"Here's what I know," Rudy said impatiently. "Otis worked for the Clyde and Davis Circus before coming here, and he got to know Mr. Barta. He picked up a few words of Mr. Barta's language, and Mr. Barta can speak a little English. A couple of weeks ago, Otis saw Mr. Barta on the street.

Mr. Barta had been worried sick about Buddy Boy and asked Otis to help him. Otis promised to leave the locks to the monkey house and the chimp cage open so that Mr. Barta could sneak through the hedge at night and grab János."

"But that plan didn't work," Stirling guessed. "So they had to try again."

Rudy nodded. "Right. The second time, Otis tried to sneak János out himself. But János bit him, and then Mr. Stephan fired Otis."

"I'm not surprised that Otis set me up," Will said. "But *you*, Rudy . . ." Although his voice was quiet, Kit saw the hurt in his eyes.

"Otis didn't tell me any of this until last night," Rudy insisted. "And I *had* to help. Buddy Boy—János—has been depressed ever since he got here. He's hardly eaten at all. I've been really worried about him."

"And you knew that Mr. Barta needed to come get János himself," Kit prompted.

"Right. So I met Mr. Barta on Vine Street, just like Otis told me to, and we slid through the hedge—"

A REUNION

"Where?" Stirling demanded. "I didn't see you."

Rudy looked startled. "Near the llama pen. Anyway, I brought Mr. Barta here and I filled a bucket with food—you know, so Mr. Barta could get a good meal into János tonight. And then we were about to go get the chimp when"—he sighed—"when everything went sour."

Officer Culpepper squinted at them, then shook his head. "I still need proof—"

Rudy stamped his foot in frustration. "I'll *show* you proof!" He grabbed Mr. Barta's arm and towed him up the steps and into the monkey house. Everyone else followed. "Wait by the chimp cage," Rudy commanded.

Kit, Stirling, Will, and the officers followed his instruction. Rudy and Mr. Barta disappeared into the workers' area behind the cages and, a moment later, appeared in the barred passageway that separated the chimps' cage from Susie's. Mr. Barta made a soft call. The chimp Kit knew as Buddy Boy loped forward, making frantic cries. When Mr. Barta entered the cage, János leapt into his arms. Kit felt a lump rise in her throat.

"Okay." Officer Culpepper held his palms up in surrender. "But what happens next'll be up to the superintendent. And I warn you, a secondhand story coming from Otis won't carry much weight."

"But Mr. Barta doesn't speak English well enough to explain everything!" Rudy suddenly looked like a little boy on the edge of tears. "Otis just kept calling him 'the foreigner.' I don't even know what country he's from."

Kit grinned. "I think I do!"

❧

"I'm not getting every word," Mrs. Dalrymple told Superintendent Stephan. "I haven't tried to speak Hungarian since my mother died. But between my poor Hungarian and his poor English, I can say that the gist of Mr. Barta's story matches what that young man told us." She nodded at Rudy. "Mr. Barta believes that

the zoo is in financial trouble. He's terrified
that his chimpanzee will be sold again."

They were all jammed in the superintendent's
office: the Kittredge family, Mrs. Dalrymple,
Miss Bravetti, Stirling, and Will; the superintendent and two Zoo Police officers; Rudy and Mr.
Barta—and János, still clinging to his old friend.
Kit was surprised to hear the sound of voices
drifting through the open windows as the last
visitors made their way toward the gate. Surely
hours had passed since she'd crouched behind
that refreshment cart!

Rudy turned toward his boss with a pleading
look. "Sir, *please* let Mr. Barta have his chimp.
I know you bought him from the circus, but
you can take his price out of my salary, a little
at a time." His face flushed. "That is, if I still
have a job here."

"I'll deal with you in a moment," the
superintendent said crisply. Kit and Stirling
exchanged worried glances.

"As for Mr. Barta . . ." Mr. Stephan pursed
his lips thoughtfully for a moment. "I recognize

him. Several weeks ago he tried to speak with me as I left the grounds. I'm sorry to say I was in a hurry, and when I couldn't understand what he was trying to tell me, I went on my way." He shook his head with regret.

Mrs. Dalrymple managed a translation for Mr. Barta, who was listening intently.

"Mr. Barta has an excellent reputation as a monkey trainer," Mr. Stephan added. "But . . . he clearly no longer has the means to care for this animal on his own."

Mrs. Dalrymple glared at the superintendent. "If you want him to hear that, you'll have to find another transla—"

"Therefore," Superintendent Stephan continued calmly, "I will have to hire him."

When she realized what Mr. Stephan was offering, Kit whooped with glee. The trainer's expression bloomed from misery to disbelief to joy as Mrs. Dalrymple managed to make Mr. Barta understand. "Yes?" he asked Mr. Stephan, gesturing around him. "I—work here?"

Superintendent Stephan laughed. "Yes, indeed. We've been short a trainer since Rudy's father died. And please tell Mr. Barta he can sleep here at the zoo until he gets back on his feet."

Mr. Barta's eyes glowed when he understood. "Thank—you," he stammered.

"Now, then. Rudy." The old man's face grew hard again. "I'm very disappointed in you. You should have come to me as soon as Otis spoke with you about all this."

Rudy hung his head. "I'm sorry, sir. It's just that . . ." He took a deep breath. "I wasn't sure you'd want to give Buddy Boy back to Mr. Barta, or could afford to. And I've been keeping a close eye on that chimp. I was afraid he was going to give up and die on us! My dad taught me that if a chimp is raised from a baby by one person, they're bonded for life."

Just like Susie and her trainer, Kit thought. Before starting this zoo adventure, she'd never known wild animals could have such deep feelings.

Superintendent Stephan looked at Rudy sadly. "Son, have you ever known me to make a decision that wasn't in an animal's best interest?"

"No, sir." Rudy sounded miserable. Kit longed to speak up on Rudy's behalf but didn't quite dare.

"There will be consequences for your actions, Rudy," Mr. Stephan said finally. "I will expect you to be first on call for the next three months if another keeper is sick."

"Yes, sir," Rudy said quickly. Kit saw the relief in his eyes.

"And I expect you to assist Mr. Barta as he gets to know the monkeys and apes. That will require extra hours as well."

Rudy looked thrilled. "Yes, sir!"

"Now to you, Will," Superintendent Stephan said. "I judged you harshly, young man, and in error. I apologize." He held out his hand.

Will returned the shake with a slow smile that *almost* seemed like the old one

Kit remembered. "I might have made the same mistake in your place, sir."

"Will came back tonight to check the building's security himself," Kit added. She wanted to be sure everyone understood his efforts.

"My timing wasn't as good as yours, though," he told her. "Good thing you gave me the danger signal, Kit. That was quick thinking."

She shrugged sheepishly. "Well, now I know there never was any real danger. But I *thought* we had a couple of unscrupulous black market monkey thieves on our hands."

"What danger signal?" Officer Culpepper asked.

"It's part of the hobo code Will taught us," Kit explained. "I chalked the 'danger' sign on the floor."

The officer rubbed his chin. "Well, I'll be."

"Thanks for letting go of my arm," she added. "If you hadn't let me run after Rudy and Mr. Barta, we wouldn't have solved this case."

The big man snorted. "I only let go because someone conked me on the head! I assume it was Will here."

"It was not!" Will protested indignantly, just as the other officer said, "It wasn't him, chief. I had a good hold of him the whole time."

They all stared at one another. Suddenly Rudy burst out laughing. "It must have been Rascal!"

Stirling looked impressed. "The baboon," he explained. "He throws things whenever he thinks someone is hurting a child. You probably got hit with a rubber ball."

"Extra treats for Rascal tomorrow," Rudy added.

Mrs. Dalrymple got to her feet. "Well, then. I think that's everything. And it's time we were all getting on our way."

"Not quite everything," Dad said, with a stern glance at Kit and Stirling. "But Mrs. Kittredge and I can take care of our business at home. We should let the superintendent and Rudy and Mr. Barta get settled in for the night."

A Reunion

"And János," Kit couldn't help adding. She hoped she and Stirling would get off as well for their part in the night's adventures as Rudy had. *But even if we don't,* Kit thought as she waved good-bye to her friends, *it was worth it.*

12
THE WHOLE STORY

"This is a great idea, Kit." Stirling hitched up the sack he was carrying. "I'm glad your parents agreed to let us take food to the hobo jungle."

Kit nodded. "After the scolding we got last week, I wasn't sure they'd let us go *anywhere* ever again. That's one Independence Day I'll never forget." A trickle of sweat ran down her neck. Even through the soles of her shoes, the sidewalk felt hot enough to fry potatoes.

"I haven't been back to the hobo jungle since Will took us two years ago." Stirling kicked a rock off the sidewalk.

Kit sighed. "It doesn't look any better now. Sometimes it feels as if this Depression is going to last forever."

"At least Mr. Barta has a new job," Stirling said.

That reminder cheered Kit up. "Yep, that worked out just fine." Five days had passed since they had discovered Mr. Barta's identity, and the Hungarian trainer was very happy with his position at the zoo.

Stirling looked at Kit. "And to think I almost missed all the excitement!" he said. "I'm glad I got worried and came to see if you were all right."

"Me too." Kit grinned at him. "If you hadn't caught Rudy, we might never have sorted out the truth." They turned a corner, and Union Station loomed into view.

"Rudy says he wouldn't be surprised if Will gets promoted to assistant keeper one day," Stirling told her. "Everyone is realizing what a good worker he is." He paused. "I just wish . . ."

Kit guessed what he was thinking. "You wish we had figured out who took the food and clothes from our house? Me too." She was relieved to learn that Will was doing so well at work. But her instincts told her that Will had not yet revealed all of his secrets, and that still hurt.

Then she squared her shoulders. "If we see Will at the hobo jungle today, I'm going to march right up, say hello, and get to the bottom of things!"

"And if we don't see Will at the jungle, maybe we can talk with him at the picnic this evening," Stirling added. "He got switched to early shift this week, and I heard him promise your dad that he'd be there."

They passed the station and rail yards, and made their way to the riverbank camps nestled among the trees. Kit and Stirling moved among the shabby tents and lean-tos, offering just-pulled carrots and vine-ripened tomatoes, Mother's biscuits, and Mrs. Dalrymple's rolls to the hungry people. "Thank you," each said, although the phrase was spoken with a variety of regional accents. "Thank you kindly."

Kit had just emptied her sack when she

suddenly grabbed Stirling's arm. "Look!" she hissed. "I think that man's wearing my dad's good suit!" She pointed to a young man sitting on an empty potato crate beside a lean-to made from planks and odd pieces of tin. He was idly whittling a stick. A fedora shielded his face from the sun.

"Are you positive?" Stirling whispered, craning to peek around a mulberry bush. "Lots of men wear dark blue suits."

"Not in the hobo jungle! Everyone else around here looks tattered, but I'll bet you a dollar that *he* hasn't hopped a train or worked in a field for quite some time!"

"You're right about that," Stirling allowed.

Kit turned to her friend with wide eyes. "We always assumed that one of the boarders took the food and my dad's suit."

"Do you think that man actually broke into our house?" Stirling looked horrified.

A ripple of unease skittered over Kit's skin. "What should we do?" she whispered.

Stirling licked his lips nervously. "I don't

think it's safe for us to go accuse him. Besides, we *promised* your parents we'd use better judgment and ask for help the next time—"

His voice broke off abruptly as a thin young woman appeared around a corner of the shelter. Sitting down beside the whittler, she gave him a beautiful smile as she slipped her arm through his.

Kit and Stirling stared at the young couple, then at each other. "Well!" Kit said finally. "I'll be a monkey's uncle!"

❧

That afternoon, Kit made her favorite salad from marshmallows, orange crescents, banana slices, crushed pineapple, and lime gelatin. Mother made a curried tuna salad, sliced radishes and tomatoes, and baked sponge cake. Mrs. Dalrymple baked *kifli* and made iced tea flavored with raspberries.

"Kit, come help me set up the table outside," Mother murmured at a moment when Mrs.

Dalrymple seemed to bustle in whatever direction Kit or Mother needed to go.

"Can we use the best crystal and china?" Kit asked. "And the nice linen tablecloth?"

Mother looked startled but then smiled. "I suppose so. Goodness! I haven't set the terrace up for a fancy party in ages!"

Not since the garden club ladies used to come, Kit thought. *Well, we'll just make this party as elegant as any garden club meeting used to be!*

By the time Dad got home from work at the airport and Mr. Peck got home from an afternoon concert, the makings of a lovely picnic supper were spread on the terrace. Miss Bravetti silently helped Mother and Mrs. Dalrymple carry trays and platters from the kitchen. Soon Stirling and Will arrived from the zoo, bringing Rudy and Mr. Barta with them.

Everyone settled around the table. Mrs. Dalrymple had just finished pouring glasses of tea when a young man walked around the corner of the house. He wore shabby clothes, but he carried a dark blue suit, folded neatly, with a fedora resting on top. "Excuse me," he said hesitantly.

"Can we help you?" Dad asked. Suddenly his questioning look turned indignant. "Hey! Is that my suit?"

"Dad," Kit said quickly, "I'd like you to meet Mr. Richards."

Miss Bravetti stepped forward. "My husband," she added.

For a moment, everyone sat in stunned silence. Then they all began chattering at once. Finally Dad held up his hands. "Quiet, everybody!" He turned to Miss Bravetti— it would take a long time for Kit to think of her as anything else—and crossed his arms. "I'd like to hear this story from you."

Miss Bravetti fingered the heart-shaped pin on her blouse. "Frank and I met more than a year ago," she explained. "He worked for an insurance company, and he volunteered to tutor some of my students who were struggling in mathematics. When we decided to marry, my parents refused to give us their blessing because Frank isn't Italian." She raised her chin. "We married anyway. My parents disowned me."

"But for heaven's sake, why all the secrecy with us?" Mrs. Dalrymple demanded.

"Because Frank lost his job, and the school board was threatening to fire married women!" Miss Bravetti said. "My little teaching income is all we have." Her voice dropped. "I was terrified we'd lose that, too."

"We couldn't pay rent, so we lost our apartment," Mr. Richards added. His handsome face was clouded with an expression Kit recognized: shame. "It's bad enough that *I'm* living in the hobo camp, but I couldn't bear my wife being there, too. So we decided to use some of her salary to pay her room and board here. Every other cent we're saving for our future."

"I'm sorry I wasn't honest with you," Miss Bravetti told Kit's parents. "And I'm especially sorry that I . . . I took some food. I know it was terribly wrong, but it was just horrible to see my husband hungry! I tried to eat less at meals to make up for it."

"And you took the suit," Mother said. Her voice was cool.

Miss Bravetti hunched her shoulders anxiously. "I just wanted to *borrow* it. I'd never seen Mr. Kittredge wear it, so I thought I could return it before anyone noticed."

"I actually had a couple of job interviews," her husband added. "My clothes have become awfully shabby, and I was afraid that not having a good suit would keep me from being considered."

"Being poor can be a terrible trap," Miss Bravetti added.

For a long moment nobody spoke. Mr. Richards took his wife's arm. "I think we should go, Angela."

"No one is going anywhere," Mother said. "I'm glad this is all out in the open. We can talk more later. For now—let's eat, everyone!"

Kit hadn't realized she was holding her breath until then. She and Stirling exchanged relieved smiles.

Everyone ate until they couldn't take another bite. "Gosh, what a great feast!" Rudy exclaimed, scooping up his last morsel of cake. "Thank you, Mrs. Kittredge. I never had such a meal."

"Thank Kit," Mother said. "The picnic party was her idea. And she helped buy the groceries."

"I didn't know that!" Dad exclaimed. "Does that mean—"

Kit bounced on her toes. "Yes! Gibb bought *both* of my articles! My story about Mr. Barta will be printed tomorrow, and my children's story about the Flying Zambinis the day after."

Everyone crowded around Kit to offer congratulations. Will hung back until the last. "Good job," he told her. "And Kit . . . thanks for all you did for me."

"You knew about Miss Bravetti, didn't you," said Kit. It wasn't a question.

Will nodded. "I saw her with Frank at the hobo jungle a few times, and once Frank came here to give his wife a message. She was terrified that I'd tell, but I promised I wouldn't."

"And you couldn't break your word." Kit nodded. "I understand that. But—but why did you keep going back to the jungle?"

"I feel at home there," Will said simply. "Your family's been nothing but kind. Still, when trouble seemed to pop up at every turn . . . I was uncomfortable here. I found a widow lady a couple of blocks away who needed help in her garden. I'd work there in the mornings, she'd pay me in vegetables, and I'd take them to the jungle and eat with the hoboes. That way I ate less food here, too."

"I wish you'd just told me. I would have understood."

"Maybe so." Will mulled that over. "I guess I've been on the road so long, I *expect* folks to think badly of me. But you wouldn't give up on me, even when I gave up on myself. I'm mighty grateful, Kit."

"I'm not giving up on trying to help other people who are down on their luck, either," Kit said earnestly. "Right now, my job is to write what the editor asks for. But I promise you, I'm still going to write about how awful it is for people who lose everything and how easy it is to help someone who's having a hard time. If Gibb doesn't want to publish those stories, I'll find someone who does."

Will grinned, the old, warm grin Kit had been longing to see. "That would be great."

"Attention, everyone!" Mrs. Dalrymple stood by the table, clinking a fork against Mother's best crystal vase. "I have a little something for Mrs. Kittredge." Mrs. Dalrymple nodded at Miss Bravetti, who stepped forward and put something large and bulky in Mother's lap.

"What on earth?" Mother blinked with surprise, then unfolded a quilt. The top was pieced from hundreds of tiny hexagons. "Why—it's lovely!"

"I managed a home of my own for almost forty years," Mrs. Dalrymple said. "And I daresay I wouldn't have liked other people coming and going all the time, always underfoot. Yet you make it seem easy, Mrs. Kittredge."

Mother looked speechless, so Kit asked, "Does this quilt have a name?"

"This pattern is usually called 'Grandma's Flower Garden,' but I'm calling this quilt 'Mrs. Kittredge's Flower Garden.'" Mrs. Dalrymple looked around the yard—past the ever-expanding vegetable garden to the now-neglected flower beds that had once been Mother's pride and pleasure. "In honor of what you've given up in order to make this boarding house feel like a true home for all of us." She smiled. "No need to thank me."

"Yes, I think there is," Mother said slowly, running her fingers over the quilt. "Thank you, Mrs. Dalrymple." She smiled at the widow. *Maybe*, Kit thought, *just maybe, Mrs. Dalrymple and Mother can become fast friends.*

Mr. Peck got out his big bass fiddle, and soon everyone was dancing the Texas two-step. Then Mr. Barta taught them all a twirling dance he called *csárdás*. By the time lightning bugs began blinking from the grass, Kit was dizzy and weak-kneed from laughter. She poured herself another glass of iced tea and plopped onto the grass beside Stirling.

"You know what the best part about living in a boarding house is?" she asked.

Stirling was tapping his fingers to the beat. "What?"

"Every single person has stories to tell." Kit spread her arms. "I don't have to look very far for *great* story ideas. They're all right here."

As music from Mr. Peck's fiddle danced through the evening, Kit started hearing another rhythm in her mind. *Clickety clack, clickety clack* . . . Her fingers itched to fly over her typewriter keys, capturing the ideas tumbling in her head. "If I work hard, maybe my dream of being a reporter will really come true someday," Kit said, as much to herself as to Stirling. "Really, really come true."

LOOKING BACK

A PEEK INTO THE PAST

When Kit was a girl, people in her hometown of Cincinnati, Ohio, liked to read about their zoo in the newspaper. Cincinnati was very proud of its zoo, which was one of the largest and oldest in America. And at a time when most newspaper

stories were about the Great Depression and workers losing their jobs, people welcomed fun stories about exotic animals and interesting doings at the zoo.

Those who could afford the 25-cent entrance fee visited the zoo. They could enjoy not only the animals and animal shows but also plays, operas, and even ice-skating exhibitions.

Programs for zoo events

On warm summer evenings, formally dressed couples could dine at the elegant Clubhouse restaurant and hear the symphony orchestra perform at the band shell. On holidays, families enjoyed picnics and concerts, just as Kit's family and friends do on Independence Day in the story.

The monkey house, where Stirling gives his tours, is the oldest zoo building still in existence in America. Today it houses the zoo's reptile collection, but in Kit's time,

The monkey house

it was famous as the home of Susie the gorilla. A star attraction at the zoo, Susie had been captured in Africa as a baby, displayed in Europe, and flown over the Atlantic Ocean to America. Susie was devoted to her trainer, just as the

Susie the gorilla and her trainer having a tea party

story's fictional chimp, Buddy Boy, was bonded with Mr. Barta. There was also a baboon who threw things from his cage whenever he saw a child being handled roughly—just as Rascal does when Officer Culpepper grabs Kit!

Sol Stephan ran the Cincinnati zoo for 51 years. He lived right next door to the zoo and spent every day there, from early in the morning until late at night. No detail escaped his sharp eye! The health and happiness of the animals were his foremost concerns. In an era when animals were usually trained with whips and fear, Mr. Stephan encouraged his keepers to talk to their animals in a friendly tone to establish trust. He was an early believer in kindness as the best way to handle animals.

Sol Stephan was an expert at handling not only animals but also people, and he inspired great loyalty among his workers. One of his employees, Ed Coyne, started working for the zoo at age ten, just like Rudy in the story, and served as the elephant keeper for 65 years. When times were hard, Mr. Stephan had been known

Sol Stephan with a baby pygmy elephant

Come Up Sometime And See Me In My Bar-less Cage

I'm home most all the time. Enjoy a wholesome day in a healthful atmosphere.

At the ZOO

LION GROTTO, (BARLESS) AT THE CINCINNATI ZOO, CINCINNATI, OHIO

Sol Stephan developed large, natural-looking enclosures for his lion and tiger exhibits. The lion grotto opened in 1934.

to give his workers money out of his own pocket. Mr. Stephan loved children and arranged for Cincinnati public schools to visit the zoo twice a year so that the students could study the animals. In 1934 he started a children's radio program, "Uncle Steph's Zoo Club." He also began the Zoo Guides program in the 1930s, with Boy Scouts leading tours of the zoo, just as Stirling does in the story.

Sol Stephan was one of the first American advocates of "barless" exhibits, stating that they were not only more attractive and educational than conventional iron and concrete cages, but also better for the animals. As early as 1913, he predicted that zoos of the future would become "barless and cageless." The tiger grotto that Kit admired was an early example of this trend, and naturalistic animal habitats are now common in zoos today. Sol Stephan's prediction was right!

A naturalistic exhibit in a modern zoo

ABOUT THE AUTHOR

Kathleen Ernst grew up in Maryland. The Baltimore Zoo turned a century old in 1967, when she was eight years old, and she has happy memories of visiting it with her family. She loved the barrel bridge in the children's area—and of course the monkeys and apes were some of her favorite animals.

Today she and her husband live in Wisconsin. She is the author of three American Girl History Mysteries: *Betrayal at Cross Creek*; *Whistler in the Dark*, which was nominated for the 2003 Agatha Award for Best Children's/Young Adult Mystery; and *Trouble at Fort La Pointe*, a 2001 Edgar Award nominee for Best Children's Mystery. She has also written several young-adult novels set during the Civil War.